GREAT STORIES

SIX DETECTIVE STORIES

Abridged and Simplified by

S.E. PACES

BLACKIE®
ELT BOOKS
(An imprint of S Chand Publishing)

BLACKIE ELT BOOKS

(An imprint of S Chand Publishing)
A Division of S Chand And Company Limited
(An ISO 9001 Certified Company)
Head Office : B-1/D-1, Ground Floor, Mohan Co-operative Industrial Estate, Mathura Road,
New Delhi–110 044; **Phone** : 011–6667 2000, **e-mail** : info@schandpublishing.com
Registered Office : A-27, 2nd Floor, Mohan Co-operative Industrial Estate, New Delhi–110 044
www.schandpublishing.com; **e-mail** : helpdesk@schandpublishing.com

Branches :

Ahmedabad	:	Ph: 079-2754 2369, 2754 1965, ahmedabad@schandpublishing.com
Bengaluru	:	Ph: 080-2235 4008, 2226 8048, bangalore@schandpublishing.com
Bhopal	:	Ph: 0755-4274 723, 4209 587, bhopal@schandpublishing.com
Bhubaneshwar	:	Ph: 0674-2951 580, bhubaneshwar@schandpublishing.com
Chennai	:	Ph: 044-2363 2120, chennai@schandpublishing.com
Guwahati	:	Ph: 0361-2738 811, 2735 640, guwahati@schandpublishing.com
Hyderabad	:	Ph: 040-4018 6018, hyderabad@schandpublishing.com
Jaipur	:	Ph: 0141-2291 317, 2291 318, jaipur@schandpublishing.com
Jalandhar	:	Ph: 0181-4645 630, jalandhar@schandpublishing.com
Kochi	:	Ph: 0484-2576 207, 2576 208, cochin@schandpublishing.com
Kolkata	:	Ph: 033-2335 7458, 2335 3914, kolkata@schandpublishing.com
Lucknow	:	lucknow@schandpublishing.com
Mumbai	:	Ph: 022-2500 0297, mumbai@schandpublishing.com
Nagpur	:	Ph: 0712-2250 230, nagpur@schandpublishing.com
Patna	:	Ph: 0612-2260 011, patna@schandpublishing.com
Ranchi	:	ranchi@schandpublishing.com
Sahibabad	:	Ph: 0120-2771 238, info@schandpublishing.com

ISBN : 978-81-21926-13-3   **Product Code:** SCS2GSE030ENGAA04CBN

PRINTED IN INDIA

By Vikas Publishing House Private Limited, Plot 20/4, Site-IV, Industrial Area Sahibabad, Ghaziabad–201 010 and Published by S Chand And Company Limited, A-27, 2nd Floor, Mohan Co-operative Industrial Estate, New Delhi–110 044.

CONTENTS

Chapter   **Page**

1. The Case of the Sharp-Eyed Jeweller 1

2. The Case of the Reigate Murder 15

3. The Case of the Missing Clock 41

4. The Case of the Camden Killer 62

5. The Case of the Stolen Letter 84

6. The Case of the Missing Plans 102

    Questions and Language Practice 130

THE CASE OF THE SHARP-EYED JEWELLER

NICOLAS BENTLEY (1907-1978) is one of the famous writers of fictions and books. He was educated at University College School and Heatherly School of Fine Arts. He considered his work as an illustrator to be only a pleasant interlude.

His present story is about a theft case. Regnier's Jewellery shop was very famous for its quality and uniqueness. The story evolves around the theft of a high price ring. Apparently the thief appears to be very sharp-minded by not leaving any clue of the theft behind him. But in the end, by the virtue of the sharp-mindedness of the shop assistant, here Nicolas himself, the ring theft mystery sets resolved and Nicolas gets rewarded by the shop owner.

1
THE CASE OF THE
SHARP-EYED JEWELLER

NICOLAS BENTLEY

First, let me introduce myself. My name is William Morris. I am a very ordinary man except that I use my eyes and my common sense more than most people do. My hobby is perhaps a little out of the ordinary. It is the study of crime and criminals. For the past thirty years I have made a study of the crime stories of the greatest authors, from Edgar Allan Poe to Agatha Christie. And here, I must say that the stories I have most enjoyed are not those where the detective is an extraordinary person, extraordinarily favoured by fortune, but where he is just an ordinary man who uses his eyes and his common sense to the full.

I love to watch people. Some men love to watch the behaviour of birds, others the behaviour of fish, but I love to watch how men and women behave. I have the habit of observing everything they do—the way they walk, speak and pray, what they eat, read, wear and wish for. Nothing ever escapes my sharp eye. Of course you cannot learn much from one fact, but, if you put two or more facts together, you can learn a great deal. I admit that I am only guessing at the truth and that my guesses may be wrong. All the same, it is an interesting pastime and I thoroughly enjoy it.

Let me give you some examples of things that I notice.

The young woman sitting opposite me in the train is crying. I look at her hands and I see on her ring-finger the mark where a wedding ring has been. It has gone now, and it seems that her happiness has gone with it.

A man has been standing at the corner of the street for the last half hour or more. He is staring at an opened newspaper, but is he really reading it ? In half an hour he hasn't turned a single page. Is he a detective watching and waiting for some particular person to enter or come out of a house nearby ? Or, is he waiting for his girl-friend ? No

I don't think so. If he were, he would have put on a better suit and have polished his shoes.

I like guessing at nationalities too. This brightens many a dull hour. When I am waiting for my lunch in a crowded restaurant where the service is slow, I never get impatient or annoyed as most people do. I just look at the people around me and ask myself, "Is he German ?" "Is she Italian or Spanish ?" "Surely that man is from the South of China ?" An American is the easiest of all to pick out. There is his hair-cut, his tie in so many bright colours, and then so often you find him chewing— chewing that dreadful chewing gum. Once I tried chewing the stuff to see what it was like. Never again!

I have told you something about my hobbies and habits and now I shall speak of my work. I am a jeweller, or more accurately, a jeweller's assistant. This may not strike you as anything important or unusual, but when I tell you that I am working for Regnier's, I am sure that you will be impressed. Everyone knows Regnier's, which is famous for antique jewellery that it sells at prices that only the very rich can afford. Our principal customers are millionaires, oil-kings, film-stars, heroes of the football field, and people of that class. The jewels we sell are never less than three hundred years old. Some of them have a romantic history. Many had once been the gifts of a prince to some reigning beauty of his time.

As for the shop itself, it is small, old-fashioned and rather dark, with an atmosphere like that of a church, quite the opposite of anything modern and showy. To the left as you go in, there is a long counter where I show the precious jewels to our wealthy clients. Behind this, there is a smaller counter where the other assistant, Miss Susskind, works. Mr. Regnier spends most of his time in his small office at the back of the shop and no one under the rank of duke will ever draw him out of it. Most of the jewellery is kept in the safe and we display only a little of it in our shop window, which is protected with iron bars.

The first thing I do when I get to work in the morning is to put in the

window some pieces of jewellery which are always kept in the safe overnight. I was doing this on that eventful day when I noticed a young woman standing in front of a shop on the opposite side of the street. Her eyes were fixed on the display in the shop window, and she stood there all the time it took me to arrange our display—quite fifteen or twenty minutes. And what do you think she was staring at ? Well, the shop is an undertaker's, and

in the window there was nothing but two urns for holding the ashes of the dead, and some photographs of grave-stones. Her interest in such things struck me as very strange. The thought crossed my mind that someone dear to her had died. Maybe. But she was not wearing black or any other sign of mourning. She was, in fact, wearing a bright yellow coat with a vivid zig-zag pattern running all over it, and yellow sandals. She had no hat on and her yellow hair reached to her narrow shoulders and spread over them most untidily. There was something of

the artist about her, I thought, but if she was an artist, she could not be a successful one. Her appearance was too shabby for that.

I had finished arranging the jewels in the window and was still keeping one eye on the young woman when a man came into our shop. It was immediately plain to me that he was an American—and one of those gum-chewing Americans. He was a big, strongly-built man, with a red face that showed he drank more than was good for him. His suit was a darkish grey but his tie was a mixture of exceedingly bright colours. I took him to be about thirty-five years old.

"Good morning, sir," I said, "May I help you ?"

"Well," he said, rolling the gum round his mouth, and speaking with a strong Yankee accent, "I'd like to look at some rings."

"Certainly, sir. Is there any particular kind you have in mind ?"

"I guess not," he said. "Just show me some."

I opened the safe and took out a tray of rings to show him and to get some idea of what he wanted. He picked out two or three of them

and asked the price of them. I noticed that he was left-handed. It was clear that he knew nothing at all about precious stones and the nature of their setting. The price was the measure by which he judged them.

There was one most beautiful ring, with diamonds and rubies set in the shape of a flower. It was well over three hundred years old and had been in the possession of a royal family. Mr. Regnier had set a very high price on it because he did not really wish to sell it. Mr. Regnier was like that. There were some of his jewels that he loved as much as he loved his children. The American preferred this flower ring to all the others but he complained that the price was too high. He asked to see some other rings and I showed him three more trays but he was still unsatisfied. His eye then fell on a fourth tray which was still inside the safe—whose door I had left open.

"I guess I'd better take a look at those, as well," he said.

I turned to take the tray out of the safe and then turned quickly back again to put the tray on the counter. It was then that I saw that the diamond and ruby ring had disappeared.

I made a sign to Miss Susskind and she came and stood beside me. Then I said to the American:

"I see that you have decided on the flower ring, sir. If you will kindly hand it to me, I will find a suitable box for it."

I held out my hand for the ring.

"I haven't decided on anything yet," the American said. "I'm not the one who's going to decide. I'm just picking out two or three rings for my wife to choose from. She'll be coming in later this morning to make her choice."

"But the flower ring! Where is it?" I asked in dismay. Then I turned to Miss Susskind.

"Will you please ask Mr. Regnier to come here ?" I said.

I came out from my side of the counter and began searching for the ring. The American joined in the search, and so did Mr. Regnier and Miss Susskind. I could see that Mr. Regnier was most upset but he was doing his best to keep calm.

Then Miss Susskind said, "I think that you ought to look in the turn-ups of his trousers."

The suggestion was a reasonable one. It is quite easy for something small to drop in the turn-up of a trouser leg. And Miss Susskind, who is a very kind person, meant him no harm, but he turned on her with a very ugly look. His face turned even redder than before, and I noticed that he had stopped chewing. His jaw moved as if he were a fierce dog ready to bite. It was a dangerous moment and I felt afraid, but Miss Susskind stood there perfectly calm. Then the American bent down and felt round his turn-ups, and I helped him to, but there was nothing there.

The American laughed. "I suppose you're thinking that I've stolen it," he said.

"Oh, no, sir. Of course not," Mr. Regnier protested, "Of course I do not suspect you. But when I report the matter to the Insurance Company, I shall have to inform them that I made a thorough search—even on you, sir, if you will excuse me."

"O.K.," said the American and went off quite cheerfully to Mr. Regnier's office where Mr. Regnier searched through his clothes—without finding any trace of the ring.

While this was happening, Miss Susskind and I were still looking for the ring, but without much hope of finding it. We were sure that it had been stolen, and by the American, but how did he do it, and where had he put it ? That was a mystery.

Another customer then came in. It was the young woman who had been looking at the funeral display in the undertaker's window for such a long time. Her coming in at this moment struck me as rather strange.

I looked at her across the counter and noticed several things. Her handbag was of an expensive kind but it was old and worn and very shabby. The same was true of her clothes. Clearly, she had been well-off once, but now she was living in poverty. She had not come here to buy anything. More likely, she had come with something to sell.

She put her handbag down on the counter and, taking a little paper packet out of it, she put that down beside her bag. She used her left hand to do this but, strangely enough, she had not shown herself left-handed in anything that she had done before. I noticed her fingers: they were short, her nails were dirty and she had no wedding ring.

I opened the packet and found inside it a piece of cheap jewellery—a filigree brooch with an imitation turquoise stone, worth about thirty shillings.

"Could you mend this for me?" she asked, showing me the broken pin of the brooch.

"I am sorry, madam," I said. "Regnier's does not do repairs."

"Thank you," she said. Then, as if by accident, her arm somehow swept against the paper in which the brooch had been wrapped, and this fell to the floor on my side of the counter. I say "as if by accident" because, in fact, it was no accident at all. It was a cunning trick.

I realised this as I bent down to pick up the paper. All the facts

suddenly came together in my head, and I knew what had happened to the flower ring. All the things that I had noticed joined to form a single picture, and that picture showed me all that I wanted to know.

I put the brooch back into its paper wrapping and handed it to her. She put it into her handbag, using her right hand to do this, and then turned to leave the shop.

"One moment, madam," I said.

She heard me but she pretended that she hadn't. She walked on towards the door.

"Pardon me," I said, "but if you don't stop, I shall press the alarm and the door will be locked."

She stopped but she did not look round.

Miss Susskind stood like a statue behind the other counter while I went up to the young woman. "Madam," I said, "we do not wish for any unpleasantness. Kindly hand me the ring which you have in the left-hand pocket of your coat. If you will not, Miss Susskind will press the alarm."

The young woman was looking deathly pale and very frightened. I felt sorry for her. Without saying a word, she felt in her pocket and gave me the ring. She ran out of the shop as if the place was on fire.

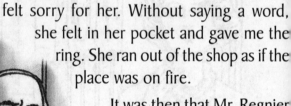

It was then that Mr. Regnier came out of his office with the American, whose face was one big grin of satisfaction. Mr. Regnier was not smiling. He was as white as a sheet. He was getting on in years and the theft of the ring that was so dear to him was a heavy blow. His voice was shaking as he said, "I am so sorry, sir. I hope that you will understand and excuse me. I beg you pardon, indeed I do."

It was then that I opened my hand and showed the ring. It is a pity that you were not there to see Mr. Regnier's face. What a mixture of astonishment, joy and thankfulness!

As for that American, he was out of the shop that instant, like a shot from a gun.

"How.....how did you find it?" gasped Mr. Regnier, falling into a chair.

"Well," I began, "from the first that fellow seemed a strange customer for us. That type of American does not come to us as a rule. They want something more modern and showy than what we sell. Besides, he didn't know a thing about jewellery and he didn't even know what he wanted. People who come to Regnier's know what they want and they generally know something about antique jewellery. And so, I said to myself, "Why has he come to us?"

"Right, quite right," said Mr. Regnier. "That was very clever of you, William."

"Then," I continued, "there was the young woman. I saw her standing about for quite a while, looking at the display opposite."

"The undertaker's?" said Mr. Regnier. "How very strange!"

"That is what I thought. And why was she waiting about all that time if she intended to come in? Why did she bring us a cheap brooch to repair? Everyone knows that Regnier's has nothing to do with cheap trinkets and never does cheap repairs."

"Certainly not," said Mr. Regnier, deeply shocked at the thought.

"Go on."

"Now, she isn't left-handed, but she took the packet out of her bag with her left hand. And she put her left hand just where the American, who was left-handed, had put his after I had taken that last tray of rings out of the safe, just before I noticed that the flower ring had disappeared.'

"And what had he done with it ?" asked Mr. Regnier.

"It was like this," I explained. "It all became clear to me when I was picking up that piece of paper. When the American looked so angrily at Miss Susskind, I noticed that he had stopped chewing his gum. Now, you can't swallow chewing-gum. You can't drop it on the floor, either. We haven't got a waste-paper basket here, and, in any case, he hadn't moved an inch from where he was standing. He must have put the gum somewhere well within his reach. Where? Where else could he have put it except under the edge of the counter ? And then he pressed the ring into the gum for the girl to take out when she came into the shop. And that is what she did. As the girl turned to go out, I found the gum just where I had expected it to be. Here it is! Look, you can see the mark that the ring made in it."

How differently people react to the same happening! Mr. Regnier was angry at the attempted theft and most grateful to me. But Miss Susskind, I noticed, only said, "Tsk, tsk". I notice that she often says "Tsk, tsk" when anything upsets her.

THE CASE OF THE REIGATE MURDER

CONAN DOYLE (1859-1930) *is among the greatest writers of detective stories. He is the inventor of that most famous detective, Sherlock Holmes, and of his faithful friend, Dr. Watson. Holmes is able to solve the deepest mysteries in original and brilliant fashion. This can be seen in the two stories in this collection:* "THE CASE OF THE REIGATE MURDER" *and* "THE CASE OF THE MISSING PLANS"

2
THE CASE OF THE REIGATE MURDER

CONAN DOYLE

It was on April 14th that I received a message to say that my friend Sherlock Holmes was ill in a hotel in Lyons, France. Within twenty-four hours I was at his bedside and was much relieved to find that he was not as ill as I had feared. He was, in fact, suffering from exhaustion. He was worn out mentally and physically by the tremendous efforts he had been making to catch the cleverest criminal in Europe. His efforts had been successful but they had resulted in a nervous breakdown. This is not to be wondered at. For two months, so he told me, he had been working for some fifteen hours a day, and more than once he had no sleep for five nights. I found him lying there, exhausted, too tired to talk, too tired even to rejoice at his success.

Somehow he found the strength to make the journey back to London, and three days later, we were back in

our flat in Baker Street. But, as a doctor, I realised that London was not the place for him in his present weak state. He needed a holiday somewhere in the country. Fresh air, fresh food and such pastimes as walking and fishing were the best medicine for him, and this was the medicine that I prescribed. I got in touch with an old friend of mine, Colonel Hayter. He had been my patient long ago when I was an army doctor in Afghanistan. He had retired and was living in a quiet little town in Surrey, a place called Reigate, one of the loveliest spots that I know. I explained the matter to him and at once he invited Holmes and me to come and stay with him for as long as it suited us. I assured Holmes that the Colonel was not married and that he would be free to do just what he liked. He then agreed to come with me. A week after our return from Lyons, we were under the Colonel's hospitable roof.

On the evening of our arrival, we were in the Colonel's gunroom, and he was showing us his collection of weapons from Asia.

"I think I'll take one of these guns upstairs with me," he said suddenly. "There may be trouble tonight."

"Trouble ?" I said in some surprise.

"Oh, yes. We've had some excitement here lately. Old Acton, a retired businessman, had his house broken into one Monday night. The thieves didn't do much damage, but the police haven't caught them yet."

"Any clues ?" asked Holmes who was immediately interested.

"None.... yet. But the robbery won't interest you, Mr. Holmes. It's only a trivial thing compared with the international crimes that you are used to."

"Was there anything peculiar about the robbery ?" Holmes asked.

"I don't think so. The thieves searched the library, and left it in quite

a mess—cupboards broken open, drawers pulled out, things thrown about—But old Acton told me that nothing of any importance was missing."

"And what actually is missing ?"

"Believe it or not, a book of poetry, two cheap candlesticks, a paper-weight, a small barometer and a ball of string."

"What a strange collection!" I said.

"Oh, the fellows just took anything they happened to lay their hands on, I expect," said Colonel Hayter.

"The local police should be able to get some clues from that," said Holmes. "It is clear that....."

I held up a warning finger.

"My dear fellow, you've come here for a rest," I told him, "and a rest you must have. You're not investigating anything until you're better. I forbid it."

"All right, Doctor Watson. All right. Keep calm," Holmes said with a smile.

My professional advice was in vain as you will see.

The subject came up again next

morning at breakfast time. We were all at table when the Colonel's butler came in, in an unusual hurry.

"Have you heard the news, sir ?" he asked in great excitement. "At the Cunninghams', sir......"

"Robbery ?" asked Colonel Hayter.

"Murder!"

The Colonel whistled. "Good heavens! Who's been killed ? The old man or his son ?"

"Neither, sir. It was William, their coachman. Shot through the heart, he was. Never spoke a word.... ."

"Who shot him ?"

"The thief, sir. He shot poor William and then ran off and got away. He had just broken in through the back door when William found him. He tried to stop him and got shot. That's how it was, sir."

"What time was this ?"

"Last night, sir, about twelve o'clock."

"We'll take a walk over there after breakfast," the Colonel said calmly. And when the butler had left the room, he went on, "It's a bad business. Old Cunningham is the biggest landowner in these parts. He'll be very upset, as William has been in his service for years. I suppose the thief or thieves were the same as those who broke into old Acton's..... ."

"And ran off with that strange collection of things," Holmes said thoughtfully.

"Exactly."

"Hm!" said Holmes. "The case may be a simple one but there is something strange about it. If the robbery is the work of a gang from outside, I should expect them to move on to another district after their first crime. It is strange that they broke into two houses, in the same place, within a few days of each other."

"I should say that it is a local thief," said Colonel Hayter. "Acton's place and the Cunninghams' are just the houses that would attract him. They are the largest in the district."

"And the richest ?" asked Sherlock Holmes.

"You would expect them to be, but actually they are not," replied the Colonel. "You see they have had a law suit for years and that has cost them a lot of money. Old Acton claims that a half of the Cunninghams' property is lawfully his, and the lawyers are still arguing about it."

"If it's a local thief," said Holmes, "the police should not find it hard to catch him." He noted my disapproving look and added hastily, "All right, Doctor Watson. I don't intend to interfere."

At that very moment the butler opened the door and announced: "Inspector Forrest, sir."

The police inspector came into the room: a heavily-built, slow-moving fellow, and I found myself wondering whether he thought as slowly as he moved.

"Good morning, Colonel," he said. "Excuse me for disturbing you, but we heard that Mr. Sherlock Holmes of Baker Street is here."

The Colonel pointed to the famous detective and the inspector bowed.

"Perhaps, sir," he said, "you would like to walk over to the house."

"Fate is against you, Watson," Holmes said to me

with a laugh. "We were discussing the crime when you came in, Inspector Forrest. Would you let us have a few details."

"We haven't a single clue in the Acton case," said Forrest. "But we have plenty in this last one. We think that the crimes are the work of the same man. And he was seen."

"Ha!"

"But he ran off after he had shot poor William Kirwan. Mr. Cunningham saw him from his bedroom window and Mr. Alec, that's his son, saw him from the back door. It was a quarter to twelve when it happened. Mr. Cunningham had just gone to bed and Mr. Alec was smoking a pipe in his room. Both of them heard William shout for help and Mr. Alec ran downstairs to see what was happening. He found the back door open, and from the foot of the stairs, he could see two men fighting outside. One of them fired, the other dropped down, and then the killer raced across the garden, through the hedge separating the garden from the road, and away. Mr. Cunningham, from his bedroom window, saw the fellow on the road but very soon he was out of sight. Mr. Alec stopped to see if he could do anything to help the wounded man, and so the killer was able to get away. All that they can tell us about him is that he was a man of medium height and built, and dressed in a dark suit."

"Did William say anything before he died ?"

"Not a word. He was shot through the heart and died instantly."

"How did William happen to be there at the time ? Was he living at the Cunninghams' ?"

"No, he lived with his mother in a small house in the grounds. I suppose he had taken a walk up to the Cunninghams' to see whether everything was as it should be. That Acton robbery gave us all a fright and we have all been extra careful since then. The thief had just broken the lock of the kitchen door when William found him."

"Did William say anything to his mother before he went out ?"

"She is old and stone-deaf. The shock has been too much for the poor soul and now she is almost out of her mind." He felt in his pocket then and brought out a scrap of paper which he handed to Holmes. "Here is something which may help us, sir. What do you think ? I found it between the finger and thumb of the dead man. The killer may have torn the rest of the sheet from him or William may have torn this bit from the killer's hand."

Holmes studied the scrap of paper with great interest.

This is how it looked:

For a while Holmes said nothing and so the policeman went on. "It mentions the exact time when poor William was killed, doesn't it ? It seems that there was an appointment, don't you think so, sir ? If so perhaps William was there to help the thief break in. Afterwards they may have quarrelled."

at quarter to twelve
learn what
maybe

"Perhaps..... perhaps there was an appointment. But this writing suggests..." He did not finish his sentence but buried his head in his hands and sat for some minutes, deep in thought. Suddenly he jumped to his feet. I was amazed at him for he looked a new man—Holmes as he was before his breakdown! All his tiredness had vanished and he was filled with fresh strength.

"This case interests me," he said. "If you will excuse me, Colonel, I will leave my friend Watson with you and go with the Inspector to the Cunninghams'. I'd like to go over the scene of the crime."

It was about an hour and a half after this that the Inspector came back—alone.

"Where is Holmes ?" I asked in surprise.

"Mr. Holmes is walking up and down in the field outside," the Inspector told us. "He wants all four of us to go up to the Cunninghams' together, now."

"To the Cunninghams?" asked the Colonel.

"Yes, sir."

"What for ?"

"I don't really know, sir," the Inspector said, with a puzzled look on his round, fat face. "He has been behaving very strangely, sir. He's

very excited. I can't understand him at all."

We went outside and found Holmes walking restlessly to and fro in the field. His hands were in his pockets and he seemed lost in thought. We waved to him and called. He came up to us then and said excitedly:

"This case is interesting, very interesting, very interesting indeed. Watson, your idea of a stay in the country has proved a great success. I have thoroughly enjoyed myself this morning."

"You have been up to the scene of the crime, I believe," said the Colonel.

"Yes. The Inspector and I have had a look round."

"Did you find anything that will help the police ?"

"I'll tell you all about it on the way there. Come on. There's no time to lose. Holmes hurried us on and explained, "First we examined the body. Yes, poor William's death had been caused by a bullet through

the heart. There was no doubt about that."

"Did you have any doubt about it ?" the Colonel asked him.

"No, but I like to test everything. Our examination of the body was no waste of time, I assure you. Then we saw Mr. Cunningham and his son—who showed us exactly where the killer had broken through the hedge after the murder. That was very interesting."

"And what do you think about the crime ?" I asked him.

"I think it's a very strange one. But our visit to the house will throw some light on the case, I'm sure. And we already have one very important clue." He turned to the Inspector and said, "Forrest, you and I both think that that scrap of paper in the dead man's hand is an important clue, the best that we have so far, isn't it ?"

"It is, Mr. Holmes, and it may help us a lot."

"It will help us a lot," said Sherlock Holmes. "The man who wrote that note was the man who brought William Kirwan to the Cunninghams' back door at a quarter to twelve. But we must find the rest of the note. It was torn out of the dead man's hand and that shows that someone was very anxious to get hold of it. And why so anxious ? Because it proved that he was the killer, he was the criminal who had planned the murder and carried it out. Now, what do you think he did with the rest of the note. I myself think that he pushed it into his pocket in such a hurry that he quite failed to notice that a bit of it was still in the dead man's hand. If only we could find the rest of the note, the mystery would be solved."

"Yes," I said, "but how can we look in the criminal's pocket before we have found the criminal ?"

"It's something that we have to think about," Holmes said, "Besides, there's something else. That note was sent to William. The man who wrote it did not himself take it to him. If he had taken it, he would have told William his message. Who brought the note to William ? Did it come by post ?"

"I've asked about that," said the Inspector, looking very pleased with himself. "William received a letter by post yesterday afternoon. The postman saw him tear the envelope up and throw it in the fire."

"That's a useful thing to know, Inspector," said Holmes. "You've done well."

Inspector Forrest seemed to swell with pride at this praise from the famous Sherlock Holmes.

It was not long before we reached the Cunninghams' house—a large, eighteenth century building with later additions, set in wooded grounds and gardens. Once it had been an impressive sight but now it had an air of neglect and even of poverty. We entered by a back gate and made for the kitchen door, where a policeman was standing on duty. The policeman opened the door for us and Holmes explained the details of the scene of the crime to us.

"It was there, at the foot of those stairs, that young Cunningham stood and saw two men struggling. And there," he pointed upwards, "Is the window where his father stood and watched the killer, who ran through the hedge at that point there. Mr. Alec ran out and knelt just here, beside the dying man. The ground here is very hard, as you see, and it

is a pity that there are no marks on it that could help us."

Two men came along the path towards us. One was an old man and the other was a young fellow with a broad smile on his face, and wearing a suit too bright in colour for such a sad occasion.

"So you've come back to collect more clues," the young man said in a mocking tone. "Haven't you got enough already ? Why," he said with a loud laugh, "I don't believe you've got a single one!"

"One we have, for certain," the Inspector said. "If we can find that....." he broke off suddenly and cried out, "Good heavens, Mr. Holmes, you're ill!"

My poor friend looked very ill, and indeed, so I thought, showed all the signs of a sudden heart attack. He gasped for breath, placed his hand over his heart and gave a terrible groan. Then he fell to the ground and lay there senseless for a while. We carried him into the kitchen and sat him in a chair, where he lay back, gasping for breath. It was most distressing to see. At length, however,

he recovered and struggled to get to his feet. "You must excuse me, gentlemen," he said. "Watson will tell you that I have been very ill. I am much better now but I still have these attacks from time to time. It is over now."

"Wouldn't you like to go home in my carriage?" asked Mr. Cunningham.

"Thank you," said Holmes, "that is very kind of you, but I am quite well now. And while I am here I should like to make certain of something."

"Oh, and what might that be?"

"I am not sure about the time when William Kirwan reached your house. Did he get there before the thief came or did he get there after him?"

"Well, my son Alec was still up, and he would have heard the thief moving about, if the thief had been there first."

"Where exactly was he sitting?"

"I was sitting in my bedroom," answered Alec.

"Which is the window of your bedroom? Would you kindly show me?"

"It's the last one on the left, next to my father's."

"The lamps were lit in both rooms, I suppose?"

"Yes."

"Don't you think that it's rather strange that

a thief should break into a house when he could see from the lights that two of the family were awake and up ?"

"Of course I think it's strange," replied the young man. "If the case were not a strange one, we shouldn't need your help, should we ?" He shot a nasty look at Holmes. "You are quite mistaken if you think that the man robbed our house before we found him. If he had done so, we should surely have found the rooms in a mess and some of the things missing."

"That depends on what the things were," said Holmes quietly. "This thief is a very strange one. Think of the extraordinary things that he stole from Acton's house. What were they ? A ball of string, two cheap candlesticks and other unlikely things."

"Mr. Holmes," said Mr. Cunningham, "we are entirely in the dark about everything. We are leaving the whole matter in your hands and we shall be glad to do anything that we can to help."

"It would help me if you offered a reward, and at once. I've already written out a notice about the reward and would be glad if you would sign it now. Fifty pounds was enough to offer, I thought."

So saying, Holmes handed a piece of paper and a pencil to Mr. Cunningham. The old man was just going to write his name when he stopped and said, "There's mistake here, I think, Mr. Holmes."

"I wrote it in a hurry," Holmes said, looking uncomfortable.

"You begin like this," old Cunningham pointed out: "At about a quarter to one on Friday morning, a thief broke into......" and so on. But the thief broke into the house at a quarter to twelve."

It was most unusual for Holmes to make a mistake in any detail and I was surprised. "He's still a very sick man," I thought sadly. The Inspector was taken aback as well. As for young Cunningham, he burst into a loud and most disagreeable laugh. The old gentleman quickly corrected the mistake and handed the paper back to Holmes.

Holmes carefully folded the paper and put it back into his pocket.

"And now," he said, "let's go over the house together and make certain that the thief did not steal anything."

First of all, Holmes examined the kitchen door which had been broken open. There were marks showing that a tool had been pushed in, and the lock had been pushed back by it.

"You don't use the bolts on the door, then ?" asked Holmes.

"No," replied old Cunningham. "We've never found it necessary."

"At what time do the servants go to bed as a rule ?"

"About ten o'clock."

"And William ?"

"About the same time as the others."

"Last night he was up very late. I wonder why ?" said Holmes very thoughtfully. He seemed to be speaking to himself and did not wait for an answer, but went on, "I should be glad if you would be kind enough to show me the rooms upstairs, Mr. Cunningham."

We walked upstairs and along the landing, where we passed the doors of several bedrooms. Holmes left us standing at the top of the stairs while he walked up and down the landing, looking round him carefully. Old Mr. Cunningham looked annoyed. He was clearly losing his patience.

"Mr. Holmes," he said, "surely this is unnecessary. This is my bedroom, here, at the top of the stairs, and here's my son's, next to it. The thief could never have come up here without us hearing him."

"I must ask you to be patient a little longer," said Holmes. "If you don't mind. I should like to look at the view from your bedroom windows. Now, first, your son's room." So saying, he entered young Cunningham's bedroom and looked not only through the windows but also all round the room.

"I hope that

you're quite satisfied." said Mr. Cunningham sharply.

"Thank you," said Holmes. "I have seen all that I want to."

"Then let me show you my room."

"If you will be so kind....."

On our way into the old gentleman's room Holmes dropped behind the others so that he and I were the last to go in. At the foot of the bed there was a small table with a glass of water on it, a water jug and a big bowl of oranges. As we passed it, Holmes suddenly bent down and pushed the table over. The glass and the jug were smashed to pieces and the oranges rolled all over the floor.

"Oh, Watson, what a clumsy fellow you are!" cried Holmes, blaming me for what had happened. I didn't mind. I knew that he was using me to further some plan of his, and so I bent down to pick up the fragments of glass and the oranges. The others were helping me when there came a cry of surprise from Inspector Forrest:

"Where's he gone ?"

Holmes had disappeared.

"Wait here," said young Cunningham. "I'll find him. He's mad in my opinion. Come on, father, let's see what the fellow is up to."

They ran out of the room, leaving the Inspector, the Colonel and me looking at one another in some bewilderment. "It seems to me," Forrest said, "that Mr. Alec is right. It may be his illness of course. He's been behaving very strangely all the morning. He....." Here he was interrupted by a sudden shout:

"Help! Help! Murder!"

It was Holmes shouting.

The three of us rushed out of the room and on to the landing. The shouts were coming from Alec's room. We ran in and were shocked at what we saw. The two Cunninghams were bending over Holmes who was lying on the floor. The younger one had his hands round Holmes's throat, trying to strangle him, while the old man was twisting his wrist. We rushed at them and pulled them off him. Holmes struggled to his feet.

"Arrest these men, Inspector," he said, breathing hard.

"On what charge ?"

"Murder. The murder of William Kirwan."

The Inspector stared at Holmes in astonishment.

"Oh, come now, Mr. Holmes, surely you don't mean to....."

"Take a look at their faces," Holmes interrupted him.

Their guilt was indeed written on their faces. The old man looked desperate while his son had the look

of a savage beast.

The Inspector said nothing, but walked to the door and blew his whistle.

"I have to arrest you," he said to the two Cunninghams. "I hope that we shall find that it's all a mistake, but......." He stopped suddenly and shouted, "Drop that!" He struck swiftly at Alec's hand and the gun that Alec was going to fire dropped to the floor.

Holmes put his foot on it. "Keep this," he said to the Inspector, "but this is what you really need." He held up a piece of paper, a corner of which had been torn off.

"The rest of the sheet!" cried the Inspector.

"Yes."

"Where did you find it ?"

"Where I expected to. I'll explain everything later on." Then Holmes turned to Colonel Hayter and me. "I think that you should both go home and have rest. The Inspector and I will have a little talk with the prisoners, but I'll be back at lunch-time. Then you shall hear the whole story."

At one o'clock Sherlock Holmes returned to Colonel Hayter's. He brought with him a thin, white-haired old man and

introduced him to us as Mr. Acton—in whose house the first crime had been committed.

"I wanted Mr. Acton to be here when I gave you the full details," said Holmes.

"I am completely in the dark about the whole affair," the Colonel said.

Holmes laughed. "Well, now you shall be enlightened," he said. "You shall have the full story of the murder.'

"From the very start," he began, "I was sure that the key to the mystery was that scrap of paper in the dead man's hand. And I was sure too that young Cunningham had the rest of the sheet. You see it was like this: if Alec's story was true, and if the killer had run off immediately after shooting William Kirwan, it could not have been the killer who had taken the paper. And, if it was not true, then Alec must have taken it because by the time his father had come downstairs, several servants were there and they saw nothing of the paper.

"I made a careful examination of that scrap of paper. Here

it is. You take a look at it, Colonel, and tell me if you find anything at all unusual about it."

"The writing looks uneven," said Colonel Hayter.

"My dear sir," Holmes protested, "it is quite plain that the writing has been done by two persons. First one wrote a word, and then the other wrote a word, and so on. Just look at the strong t's in "at" and "to" and compare them with the weak ones in "quarter" and "twelve". Surely you can see that the "learn" and the "maybe" are in the stronger writing and the "what" in the weaker."

"Yes, of course," agreed the Colonel. "It's all quite plain to me now. But what a strange way to write a letter! I wonder why they did it."

"They were planning a crime," said Holmes, "and each had to have an equal share of the guilt. The leader was the one who wrote the stronger letters."

"How do you know that ?" asked the Colonel, deeply interested.

"Examine the paper carefully and you will see that the man with the stronger handwriting wrote all his words first and left spaces for the other to fill in. Sometimes he did not leave enough space so that the second man had to write his letters

close together to get them all in. Look at his "quarter" between the "at" and the "to". You can see how cramped it is. Oh, there is no doubt that the man who wrote his words first is the man who planned the whole crime. Besides this," Holmes went on, "you may or may not know that a man's handwriting tells us something about his age. If we look at the bold, strong handwriting of one of the men and compare it with the weak, uncertain handwriting of the other, we can say that the former was the work of a young man and the latter the work of an old man. You can still make out the old man's writing but you will notice, for example, that he sometimes forgets to cross his "t's"."

"Absolutely right," cried Mr. Acton, who was much impressed by what Holmes was saying.

"And there's another interesting point," said Holmes. "The two sets of handwriting are the work of blood-relations. Look at their "e's". They both write with the Greek "e". And there are other facts to prove this. Well, naturally, all this led me to suspect that the Cunninghams, father and son, had written this letter."

"The Inspector took me over to the Cunninghams' house and we went over the scene of the crime. First I examined the dead man's wound and there I found something interesting. The wound was caused by a shot fired from a gun at a distance of more than four yards. The gun was not fired close to the man, in the course of a struggle, as Alec Cunningham had said. If it had been, there would have been a mark of burnt powder on the dead man's coat. There was no such mark. Young Cunningham had lied. And both he and his father had lied when they said that they had seen the killer as he escaped on to the road through a certain part of the hedge. I examined the spot they pointed out to me. There's quite a wide ditch there, with mud at the bottom of it. If the killer had crossed it, he would have left foot-prints. There were none.

The Cunninghams were liars, both of them. The unknown killer was an invention of theirs to hide their own guilt."

"And now," said Sherlock Holmes, "we come to the question of motive. What motive could the Cunninghams have for their crime? But, first of all, what motive was there for the first crime, the robbery at Mr. Acton's? The Colonel had told me of a law suit that had been going on for some time between you, Mr. Acton, and the Cunninghams. This led me to think that they had broken into your library to steal some papers which were very important in the case."

"You are right," said Mr. Acton. "I have a claim to a half of their property. If they had stolen the papers, I should not have been able to prove my claim."

"And when they did not find the papers," said Holmes, "they tried to make their search look like an ordinary robbery, and carried off anything they happened to lay their hands on. Oh, that was quite clear to me. Now I needed just one thing more to solve the mystery—the missing part of the message sent to William. Alec had snatched it from his hand—of that I was certain. Where had he put it? Where was the most likely place? I decided that it was the pocket of the dressing

gown that he had on at the time. My task was to find out if it was still here. For that purpose I asked you all to come with me to the Cunningham's place."

"My purpose, of course, had to be kept a secret from the Cunninghams. If they had known of it, they would have destroyed the paper. When the Inspector was going to mention it, I had to stop him somehow, and so I pretended to have a heart attack."

The Colonel gave a hearty laugh. "You should have been an actor, Mr. Holmes," he said. "You did it so well that you deceived all of us, even Doctor Watson. And do you mean to say that it was all a trick?"

"Yes," said Holmes with a smile. "And when I 'recovered', I tricked old Cunningham into writing the word 'twelve' so that I might compare it with the writing in the note. After that, you will remember, we went upstairs. In Alec's room I saw what I was looking for—his dressing gown, which was hanging up behind the door. We passed into old Cunningham's room and there I upset the table and sent water and oranges flying. That was another of my tricks. I did it so that I could leave you for a moment without being noticed. I ran into Alec's room, felt in the pockets of his dressing gown and found the paper. It was at that moment that the Cunninghams came in and made their murderous attack on me. If you hadn't come in so quickly, they would have killed me. I can still feel that young fellow's hands round my

throat. And his father nearly broke my wrist, twisting it to snatch the paper back."

"After you'd gone," said Holmes, "I had a talk with old Cunningham about his motive for murdering William. At first he denied everything but when he saw the proofs that I had of his guilt, he broke down and made a full confession. This is what he told me. He said that William had seen him and Alec break into Acton's house on the night of the robbery. William had told them that if they didn't pay him to keep his mouth shut about it, he'd go to the police and tell them what he'd seen. They had to agree to his demands, but Alec thought of a way out. He planned the murder of William in such a way that it would look like the work of thieves. There was a lot of talk about thieves at the time, you know. And so old Cunningham and his son wrote a note to William asking him to come to the house, and there Alec shot him. If Alec had snatched the whole of the note from the dead man's hand, they would probably not have been suspected."

"And what did the note say?" I asked

Sherlock Holmes then showed us the piece of paper which he had taken, at such risk, from the pocket of Alec's dressing gown.

This was it :

"A trick, as I expected," said Sherlock Holmes, "and quite a clever one. We don't know what was going on between William and Annie Morrison, but the Cunninghams did, and used it as a trap," he turned to me and said with a smile:

"Watson, I think your idea of a quiet rest in the country has been a great success, and I shall be feeling much stronger on my return to Baker Street tomorrow."

If you will only come round to the East gate you will will very much surprise you and be of the greatest service to you, and also to Annie Morrison. But say nothing to anyone upon the matter

THE CASE OF THE MISSING CLOCK

DOROTHY SAYERS (1893-1957), *translator, dramatist and poet, is one of the best women-writers of detective stories. Most of these concern the detective of her invention, Peter Wimsey. The best of them are "MURDER MUST ADVERTISE" and "THE NINE TAILORS." The short story "THE CASE OF THE MISSING CLOCK" is in humorous vein and has an ending which cannot fail to surprise the reader.*

3
THE CASE OF THE MISSING CLOCK

DOROTHY SAYERS

Mr. Montague Egg was a travelling salesman working for the firm of Messrs. Plummet and Rose, wine merchants. He was exceedingly good at his job, for he was determined, hard-working, patient, hopeful and cheerful. In addition to all this, he had learnt by heart most of the wise sayings in the Salesman's handbook—which contained everything that a good salesman ought to know.

On the morning of Saturday, June 18th, Mr. Egg was driving along the main road to the pretty sea-side town of Beachampton. He was out to get a fresh customer for his firm, a certain Mr. Pinchbeck who lived all by himself in a lonely cottage in a turning off the main road. Mr. Pinchbeck was a wealthy man, who, so people said, "had bags and bags of money under his bed". "Just the sort of customer we want," Mr. Egg thought with some satisfaction. It would not be easy to get him: Mr. Pinchbeck was as well-known for his unwillingness to spend as he was for his wealth. Other salesmen had told Mr. Egg that he would only be wasting his time if he tried to persuade

Mr. Pinchbeck to buy his wine and spirits. All the same, Mr. Egg was hopeful. "Who knows ?" he said to himself. "It may turn out well. What does the Salesman's Handbook say ?—"Don't let the smallest chance slip by. You never know until you try."—Well, he was going to try. He hummed a little song as he drove cheerfully along.

It was a lovely morning and there was a holiday feeling in the air. The road was filled with cars taking families for outings to the beach at Beachampton or to Melbury Woods. Mr. Egg turned off the main road when he came to the sign-post marked "Hatchford Mill", for that was the turning that

ed to Mr. Pinchbeck's cottage. Here there was no traffic at all and the silence was broken only by the noise of Mr. Egg's motor. "Mr. Pinchbeck must be exceedingly fond of peace and quiet" thought Mr. Egg as he drove along the peaceful, silent, country-road.

He had driven about a mile and a half without meeting a soul on the way when he caught sight of a small cottage standing in the middle of a neglected field. He pulled up at a broken gate and got out of his car. The cottage was a small one and looked badly in need of painting and repairing. To judge from the outside appearance of the cottage,

Mr. Pinchbeck, certainly, did not look like a possible customer! But Mr. Egg found comfort in another saying in his Handbook—"If you are a salesman worthy of the name, you can sell ice to Eskimos". "I haven't come all this way for nothing," he said to himself as, with great difficulty, he pushed open the broken gate. He then got back into his car and drove forward down the rough track that led to the front door of the cottage.

Mr. Egg knocked loudly on the front door but no one came to answer it. That often happened and he was not at all surprised. He walked round to the back of the house and knocked at the back door. Again there was no answer. Was Mr. Pinchbeck out ? Long experience had taught Mr. Egg that people often pretended to be out when an unwelcome visitor, especially a salesman, came to the door, and so, instead of going away, he stepped quietly to the window and looked in. What he saw gave him a dreadful shock. He walked to the back door, pushed it open and went inside.

A horrible sight met his eyes. Mr. Pinchbeck was lying on the floor with his head beaten in. Mr. Egg had fought in the last war and had seen many horrors, but all the same, he now felt sick. He hastily covered the body with the table-cloth. Then, because he was an orderly person, he looked at his watch. The time was exactly ten twenty-five. He took a quick look in the other rooms, the garden and the garage, and went back to his car. He drove off to the nearest police station, at Beachampton, as fast as he could go.

An inquiry into the murder took place the next day. Mr. Egg and the police gave evidence. The verdict was that Mr. H u m p h r e y Pinchbeck had been murdered by some person or persons unknown.

The police at once set to work on finding the murderer. Mr. Egg read the newspapers with unusual interest, eager to learn what the police had been able to discover. At first there was no definite news. Under the heading—

THE PINCHBECK MURDER

The "Daily News" of June 22nd reported the following:

"The murderer of Humphrey Pinchbeck, the lonely old man who was brutally beaten to death in his cottage near Beachampton, is still at large. However, the police have received certain information and hope to make an early arrest."

Three days later, this message was printed in all newspapers and given on the wireless and the television:

"The police are anxious to find the whereabouts of a man who was seen driving a sports car, number WOE 1313, in the Beachampton district at about ten o'clock on the morning of Saturday, June 18th. The man has a red beard and was wearing a grey check suit. Any person who has information to give should at once get in touch with the police at the nearest police station."

The man with the red beard and the sports car was found within two weeks of the murder. He was charged with the crime, and the date of his trial was fixed. Mr. Egg who was looking for new customers three hundred miles away, was summoned to attend the trial. He was, of course, a very important witness.

Mr. Egg saw the accused man for the first time at his trial. The man gave his name as Theodore Barton and his age as forty-two. He said that he was a poet by profession, but he did not look at all like a poet—thought Mr. Egg. He was a tall, broad-shouldered, strongly-built man and could easily have been taken for a heavyweight boxer in his younger days. The lower part of his face was hidden under a thick red beard

and moustache. The upper part was attractive though Mr. Egg did not care for the bold look in his eyes. He showed no sign of fear or nervousness although the charge against him was that of murder, and the punishment for that crime was imprisonment for life.

The judge entered the court and the trial began.

First of all, the police gave evidence about the finding of the body. A police doctor described the nature of the wounds that led to the death of Humphrey Pinchbeck. Then Mr. Egg was called to the witness-box.

In answer to the questions that were asked him, Mr. Egg stated that the time when he found the body was exactly ten twenty-five on Saturday, June 18th. The body was still warm. The front door was locked: the back door was shut but not locked. The kitchen was in great disorder, as if a violent struggle had taken place; and there was a blood-stained poker on the floor beside the dead man. Before going to get the police, he had searched the house to see if anyone was hiding there. There was no one. Nor was there anyone in the garden or in the garage. In a bedroom upstairs, he had seen a small iron chest, standing open and empty, with the keys hanging down from the lock. In the garage, he had seen some fresh oil-stains, showing that a car had been standing there only a short while ago. On the table in the sitting-room there were the remains of breakfast for two persons. No one had passed him on the road leading to the cottage, nor had he seen anyone on that road. After he had discovered the body, he had spent five minutes, or perhaps a little more, looking round the cottage, and then he had driven to the police-station by the way he had come.

At this point, Police Inspector Ramage, went into the witness-box to explain to the judge and the court something about the roads in the neighbourhood of Pinchbeck's cottage.

"The turning off the Beachampton road, that Mr. Egg drove along, passes the cottage and goes straight on for another half a mile to

Hatchford Mill. There it bends back to join the main road again at a point that's about three miles nearer the village of Ditchley."

The next witness was a baker, named Bowles. He told the court that he had called at the cottage, as he did every day except Sunday, to deliver two loaves of white bread. The time was ten fifteen. He had knocked at the back door and Mr. Pinchbeck himself had opened it. The old gentleman looked all right but he was in a bad temper. He had seen no one else in the kitchen, but, before he had knocked at the door, he had heard two voices shouting angrily at each other. He was sure that one of the voices was that of Mr. Pinchbeck but the other he had never heard before. He would say that the two men were quarrelling.

The baker's boy who was delivering the bread with him also said that he had heard two men quarrelling and he had seen a man's shoulders move across the kitchen window. The shoulders were too broad to be Mr. Pinchbeck's.

The next witness was Mrs. Chapman from Hatchford Mill. She told the court that she went to Mr. Pinchbeck's cottage every day except Sunday to do the cleaning. She always arrived there at half past seven in the morning and left at nine o'clock. On the morning of Saturday, June 18th, she got there at her usual time and found that the old gentleman had a visitor who had arrived unexpectedly the night before. She pointed to Mr. Barton and said:

"He was the visitor. I'll take my oath on it."

The visitor had slept that night on the couch in the sittingroom and—so the old gentleman had told her—he was going to leave that morning, after breakfast. She had seen his car in the garage: it was a small sports car, and she'd always remember the number because it was such an unlucky one— WOE 1313. She had got the breakfast ready for the two gentlemen. The milkman and the postman had called at the house while she was getting it ready. No one else had called while she was there. She had never known Mr. Pinchbeck to have a visitor before. She had been working for him for the last five years and he had never had a visitor in all that time. Mr. Pinchbeck and his visitor did not quarrel while she was there but she noticed that the old gentleman was in a bad temper—worse than usual.

Mrs. Chapman left the witness-box and her place was taken by Thomas White, a teenager, Mrs. Champman's sister's son, who had come from London to stay at the Mill for a holiday. He said that he had been cleaning his motor-cycle in the yard when he had heard a car with an unusually powerful engine driving along the road. He had run to the gate to get a glimpse of it because he wanted to see what kind of car it was—a sports car, for certain, and they didn't often get sports cars passing by. He did not see the car because the trees by the roadside blocked his view. He did not know what time it was then. It was after his aunt had come home because she had given him his breakfast. He'd had his breakfast, listened to some "pop" music and then his uncle had made him go out and clean his motor-cycle. Perhaps it was about ten o'clock.

The statement which Barton had made at the time of his arrest was then read out in court. He said that he was the nephew of the dead man and had spent the night at his cottage. His uncle had seemed pleased to see him. He had not seen his uncle for more than five years. He had written to him during that time but his uncle had not answered his letters. He had visited his uncle to ask him for a small loan but his uncle had shown himself very unwilling to lend him any money. He had told him to change his profession—his uncle had always been against him because he was a poet. After a time his uncle had become more reasonable and had said he would lend him some money. He went to that old iron chest of his, unlocked it and took out ten five-pound notes which he gave to his nephew. This had happened after Mrs. Chapman had left the cottage. He could not be certain of the time but probably it was then about nine forty-five. He had not quarrelled with his uncle. On the contrary, they had parted on friendly terms. He had left the cottage at ten o'clock, or very soon after that. He had driven past Hatchford Mill, on to Ditchley and then to Beachampton. There he had handed the car over to his friend—from whom he had borrowed it. He had hired a motorboat and gone over to France for a fortnight's holiday. He had no idea that his uncle was dead until Inspector Ramage came to see him with the incredible news that his uncle had been murdered and that he was suspected of the crime. He had hurried back to England at once to face the charge and to prove that he was not guilty.

Inspector Ramage was then called to the witness-box to answer questions put to him by Mr. Barton's lawyer. Mr. Egg was listening very attentively and was slow to realize what was happening just behind him. Someone was breathing very hard into the back of his neck. He turned round and found himself face to face with an elderly lady who seemed ready to burst with excitement.

"Oh!" she cried, jumping up and down in her seat. "Oh dear, what shall I do ?"

"Please, excuse me," said Mr. Egg politely, "I'm afraid I'm blocking your view."

"Oh! Oh, no! It's not that. Please, will you tell me what I ought to do ? There's something important that I really must tell them. That poor man isn't guilty at all. I know he isn't. Oh, what shall I do ? I've never been in a place like this before, and I have to tell them. If I don't they'll find him guilty, and it'll be my fault. Please, please, stop them. He didn't do it. He wasn't there. Oh, please do something about it!"

The lady was quite hysterical. She was so upset that Mr. Egg stood up and called to the judge :

"Excuse me, sir, but there is a lady here who says that she has some very important information to give to the court."

The judge looked hard at the lady. So did the jury, the lawyers, the accused, everyone, in fact. As for the lady, she blushed to the very roots of her hair, stood up and dropped her handbag. "Oh dear," she said, "I'm so very sorry. I see that I ought to have gone to the police."

Barton's lawyer came up to the lady and they

spoke together in whispers. The lawyer looked very pleased and then asked the judge :

"My lord, this lady, whom I have never seen before, has a statement to make, and I beg you to allow her to make it. It is of the greatest

Six Detectives Stories • 53

importance to the accused. It is, in fact, a complete answer to the charge brought against him."

The judge nodded, and the lady was then led into the witness-box. There she gave her name as Miss Millicent Adela Queek.

"I am an art teacher at Woodbury High School for Girls," she began. "I am always free on Saturdays and on that particular Saturday I decided to go out to Melbury Woods to do a little sketching. I started out in my car at about nine-thirty. It took me about half an hour to reach Ditchley—perhaps a little less—but I always allow myself plenty of time; I never drive fast—it's so very dangerous on the roads nowadays. When I got to Ditchley, I turned right and drove along the main road that goes to Beachampton. After a while, I began to wonder if I had enough petrol in the tank. Well, I thought I'd better stop at the nearest garage and fill up. I can't tell you exactly where the garage was but it

was on the Beachampton road and quite a distance from Ditchley. It was one of those really ugly garages that seem to spring up overnight— put together out of sheets of iron and painted a most horrible red.

"I stood there waiting while the man at the garage filled my tank, and it was then that I saw this gentleman—Mr. Barton, over there—drive up in his car. He was coming from the direction of Ditchley and driving rather fast. He stopped on the left-hand side of the road—just opposite to where I was standing and I saw him clearly. I am certain it was he. He had the same red beard and was wearing the same check suit that he has on now. Besides, there was the number of his car. Such a strange number! WOE 1313! Well, I saw him open the bonnet of his car and look inside. I suppose he found that everything was all right because he drove on, without calling at the garage."

"What time was that ?" asked Barton's lawyer.

"I can tell you exactly. You see, while I was standing there, I looked at my watch and found that it had stopped. It's done that before. Most annoying, isn't it ? I looked up at the garage clock which was just above the entrance, and this showed ten twenty. So I set my watch by that I went on to Melbury Woods. It was fortunate that I looked at the clock when I did because, later on, my watch stopped again. But I know for certain that this gentleman stopped at the garage at ten twenty. And so he could not have murdered poor Mr. Pinchbeck between ten fifteen and ten twenty-five because the Pinchbeck cottage is at least twenty miles away—more, I should think."

"And why did you not go to the police earlier ?"

"Well, you know, when they gave that message on the wireless, thought that it must be the same car as the one I had seen. But I could not be sure that it was the same man, could I ? And, naturally, for the sake of the school, I didn't want to get mixed up in a case of murder. Parents, you know, don't like it. And so, I thought I'd better see this gentleman for myself, and then I should be certain."

Inspector Ramage then requested the judge to stop the trial and give the police time to make inquiries concerning the information that Miss

Queek had given. The request was granted, and the trial was postponed for the day.

Inspector Ramage asked Miss Queek to go with him, his sergeant and Barton's lawyer to show them the garage where she had seen Barton that Saturday morning. Then he found that the police car was too small to hold all the passengers comfortably, and turning to Mr. Egg, he asked in a friendly way :

"I wonder if you would be so kind as to give me a lift ?"

"With pleasure," replied Mr. Egg. "It's a good idea of yours. If we are in the same car, you can keep an eye on me. Because if Barton didn't do it, it looks to me as if I must have done it."

The inspector smiled. He could not help it, for Mr. Egg had read his thoughts exactly. "I wouldn't say that, sir," he said.

"I couldn't blame you if you thought I was guilty," said Mr. Egg, and he smiled as a sentence from the Salesman's Handbook came into his head. "A cheerful voice and a cheerful look put orders in the order book". He got into his car and drove behind the police car along the road from Beachampton to Ditchley.

After a while, Inspector Ramage said, "We should be getting near

the place now. We're ten miles from Ditchley and I should say about twenty-five from Pinchbeck's place. Miss Queek says the garage is on the left-hand side of the road. He leaned to look out of the window on his left and cried, "They're stopping. This looks like it."

The police car in front had stopped at an ugly looking garage, put together out of sheets of iron and painted red, just as Miss Queek had told them. Mr. Egg pulled up.

"Is this the garage, Miss Queek ?"

"Well, I don't know. It looked just like this, and it was about here. But I don't feel sure." She looked round her and up where the clock should be. "No!" she cried. This isn't it. There isn't a clock. There ought to be one, up there, over the entrance. I'm so sorry I made such a silly mistake."

"We'll drive on," said Inspector Ramage. "It can't be far off."

The two cars moved on for another five miles, and then stopped again. Surely there was no mistake this time. The garage was just as Miss Queek had described it—ugly and bright red and put together out of sheets of iron. The clock over the entrance pointed correctly to seven fifteen.

"I feel certain that this must be it," said Miss Queek. "Oh yes, and there's the man who served me with petrol," she said as the owner of the garage came out to see what they wanted.

Inspector Ramage questioned the man.

"Did you serve this lady with petrol on Saturday, June 18th, at about ten twenty in the morning ?"

"I can't say that I remember serving her, sir. I've served so many

drivers since then. Of course, if the lady says so, then perhaps I did."

"Does your clock keep good time ?"

"Perfect, sir. It's never been out of order since it was first put in, and that was nearly three years ago."

"And if your clock pointed to ten twenty, would you swear that the time was ten twenty."

"I would, sir."

"Did you see on that Saturday morning a car with the number-plate NOE 1313 ?"

"No, sir, I can't say that I did. Of course if it had come into the garage, I might have noticed it. We get a lot of drivers stopping on the road nearby to look at their motors in case something is out of order and they need repairing. On a Saturday morning there would be too many for me to notice any particular one."

"I am quite certain that this was the place and he was the man and here's the clock," said Miss Queek.

"We'll go on as far as Ditchley to make certain," said Inspector Ramage. "There may be other garages that look the same as this."

They drove on to Ditchley but saw no other garage that looked the same. The colour was different, the size was different, the owner was different, or there was no clock.

"Well," said Inspector Ramage, "this proves that Barton is not guilty. He can't be. Look at the facts. The garage where Miss Queek saw him is eighteen miles from Pinchbeck's cottage. Pinchbeck was alive at ten fifteen when, as we know, he spoke to the baker. How could Barton cover the eighteen miles in five minutes—unless he was driving at over two hundred miles an hour? Impossible! Ah well, we'll have to make inquiries somewhere else."

"It's beginning to look as if I murdered him," said Mr. Egg calmly.

"I don't think so," Ramage said. "The baker and the baker's boy heard two men speaking in the kitchen, and it sounded as if they were quarrelling, you remember. You could not have been there with Pinchbeck because I've checked your movements and the times you gave me," he ended with a smile. "Well, I think we'd better start back."

Mr. Egg was thinking hard as they drove back. He did not say a word until they had passed the garage with a clock, the one where Miss Queek had seen Barton, then he gave a sudden cry and stopped the car.

"What's the matter ?" asked the inspector.

"An idea!" cried Mr. Egg joyfully. "I've just had a bright idea." He took a small diary out of his pocket and studied it. "Ha! Just as I thought," he said. "I've discovered something most, most interesting. Do you mind if I stop and check it ?"

"Not at all, " said Ramage, "but I'm in the dark. Please explain."

"All in good time," said Mr. Egg happily. 'What does the Salesman's Handbook say? "Don't trust to luck, but be exact and check the very smallest fact". That's what I'm going to do." He put the diary back in his pocket and drove  on. The police car was now some way ahead of him but he caught up with it. They soon reached the garage where they had first stopped, the one that answered Miss Queek's description except that it had no clock. Mr. Egg pulled up in front of the garage and shouted to the police car to stop. They all got out.

The owner of the garage came towards them to see what they wanted. All of them were instantly struck by the close resemblance between him and the man in the second garage, the one with the clock.

"Why!" cried Mr. Egg, "you look just like the man farther down the road."

"Not surprising. He happens to be my brother."

"Your garages look alike, as well."

"Yes. We bought them from the same firm, that is, we bought the pieces and put them up ourselves. It's a fairly easy job and it saves a lot of money."

"The only difference is that your brother has a clock, and you haven't."

"That's right. But I'll be getting one soon. I've already ordered one and it should come any day now."

"And you've never had a clock ?"

"Never."

"Have you seen this lady before ?" Inspector Ramage asked, pointing to Miss Queek.

The man looked hard at the lady. "I believe I have," he said. "Didn't you come in for petrol one morning, Miss. It'd be about two Saturdays ago. I think it was you. I can't remember names but I've got a good memory for faces."

"What time was it ?"

"About ten to eleven. I'm sure of that, sir because I always have a cup of tea at eleven and start boiling the water at ten to..... I was jus filling the kettle when she came."

"Ten to eleven," said the inspector. "And this is.... ." he though

or a moment.... "just twenty two miles from Pinchbeck's cottage. Half
in hour from the time of the murder. Forty-four miles an hour. He could
lo that easily in that sports car of his."

"But this can't be the place. It's never had a clock. The man said
.o, himself" said Barton's lawyer.

"Just a minute." said Mr. Egg. He turned to the owner of the garage
and asked him, "Didn't you have one of those clock-faces with movable
hands to show lighting-up time ?"

"Yes, I did," the man said. "As a matter of fact, I've still got it." It
used to hang over the entrance but I took it down last Saturday or
Sunday—last Sunday it was. It was a nuisance because so many people
ook it for a real clock."

"Lighting-up time on June 18th," said Mr. Egg softly, "was at ten
wenty, so my diary tells me."

"Mr. Egg, it's very clever of you to think of that," said Inspector
Ramage.

"Very clever indeed," said Mr. Egg cheerfully. What does the
Salesman's Handbook say ? "The salesman who uses his brain, will save
himself a world of pain."

THE CASE OF THE CAMDEN KILLER

AUSTIN FREEMAN *is the inventor of the well-known Dr Thorndyke, a detective of a modern kind who uses his knowledge of Science and Medicine in his successful search for criminals. "THE CASE OF THE CAMDEN KILLER" shows Thorndyke at work and Freeman at his best.*

4

THE CASE OF THE CAMDEN KILLER

AUSTIN FREEMAN

I myself am a doctor, a Doctor of Medicine, and my chief interest is, of course, my work but I am also deeply interested in crime and criminals. That does not mean that I am a detective in my spare time. Oh, no, though I have to admit that from time to time I have helped in the solving of mysteries that have baffled the police. The fact is that I am a great friend and admirer of the famous detective, Doctor Thorndyke. Doctor Thorndyke, I should explain, is more than a Doctor of Medicine. He is a Doctor of Science, as well. His deep knowledge of these two sciences has been a great help to him in the investigation of crime. His use of science in tracing criminals has brought him international praise and fame. Doctor Thorndyke is my friend and he has often allowed me to accompany him on his investigations. I am honoured by his friendship and proud of it when I think of his great talent and my own lack of it.

I would like to give you some idea of how he used his talent and so I shall tell you how he solved the case of the Camden killer—the brutal murderer who killed four men in the short space of six months. His first murder was in Camden and from this he was given his nickname. His last was in Bloomsbury and for this he was given a life sentence in prison.

Thorndyke and I were strolling one day through Blooms bury and I was telling him how fond I was of that part of London. I had lived there in my student days and had much enjoyed the mixture of people, students in particular, who had their homes or their lodgings there.

"Such an interesting crowd!" I said. "Indians, Africans, Japanese, but Indians most of all."

At that very moment, an Indian came running down the street towards us. He was well-dressed but hatless and he was stopping to look anxiously at each name-plate he passed.

"Can you tell me where I can find a doctor?" he asked us breathlessly.

"I am a doctor," Thorndyke told him.

"Oh, please come with me. My poor brother.....He's dying."

We followed the Indian to his brother's flat in the next street. On the way he gave us some details, as well as he could, for he was breathing hard and trembling like a leaf from shock.

"My name is Byramji," he said. "When I entered my brother's house, he was lying on the floor, in the sitting room, gasping for breath. I spoke to him but he didn't answer. Oh, hurry, please."

"The poor fellow's had a heart attack," thought I, "and is probably dead by now."

It looked as if I were right. We found the man lying there and breathing hard. His eyes were still open. I bent down to feel his heart-beats. They were very weak and growing weaker and weaker. They stopped. I stood up.

"He's dead," I said. "I'm sorry. It was his heart."

"No," said Thorndyke. He bent down to touch the man's right ear and showed us his fingers. They were red with blood. He passed his hand very gently over the man's head.

"He died of a heavy blow on the head," he said. "He's been murdered."

I must confess that I felt very upset when I heard that. As for Byramji, he looked as if he were

going to drop down in a faint. However, he found enough strength to answer Thorndyke's questions.

"Who was in the house when you came in ?" the detective asked him.

"No one, but the landlady was in her flat downstairs, I think. I heard the television as I came upstairs."

"Ask her to come here."

But the landlady could tell them

nothing. She and her little boy had been watching a football match on the television and had seen and heard nothing but what was happening on the football field.

"Was your brother expecting a visitor this afternoon ?"

"Yes, a buyer was coming to discuss the price of a ruby that my brother was going to sell."

"And who was this buyer ?"

"I'm sorry. I have no idea. My brother didn't tell me."

"And your brother had a ruby to sell ?"

"Yes. My brother brought it back with him from Burma. It was the largest ruby that I have ever seen, and

worth a fortune, I should think. He always carried it about with him, in a leather bag round his neck." He bent down and searched. "It's gone!" he cried. "The ruby is gone!"

We searched on the floor and found the leather bag not far from he body. It was empty, of course. I found someone's hat near a leg of the table.

"Whose hat is that ?" Byramji asked.

"Isn't it your brother's ?"

Byramji took the hat and examined it. "It looks a lot like his but it isn't his. I know his well because it's just the same as mine. His is lined with white silk and there's a leather band round the crown with his initials on it—D.B.—in gold letters. This one has no silk lining and no gold lettering. It isn't my poor brother's."

"It must be his visitor's—the killer's," I said.

Thorndyke placed the hat on the dead man's head and we saw that it fitted him quite well.

"Ha!" said Thorndyke, "I can see what happened. The visitor put his hat on the table beside your brother's, Mr. Byramji. They sat down to have a talk about the ruby. The discussion became a quarrel and then there was a struggle. It was during the struggle that the visitor's hat was knocked off the table. But the struggle was a brief one because the killer had his weapon ready, you can be sure. Then, when your poor brother lay dying at his feet and the ruby was safe in his pocket, the

killer hurried off. In his hurry, he picked up the only hat that lay on the table and put that on. The size was all right for him."

Thorndyke was looking at the hat, inside and outside. He looked up and said to me, "Send the landlady's boy for the police, will you? But before they come, I'd like to make a thorough examination of the hat. I have a feeling that it has a lot to tell us. Mr. Byramji, have you a small, hard brush that you could let me have ?"

Byramji brought him a brush and Thorndyke brushed the outside of the hat over some newspaper spread out on the table. He collected the dust that had fallen on the newspaper and put it into an envelope, writing on the envelope "outside of hat."

He then examined the inside of the hat. Under the leather band, he fond some pieces of paper which had been put there to make the hat a closer fit. Most were pieces torn from a newspaper and Thorndyke studied them carefully. One of them was part of a price-list of gasheaters and furnaces. Another was part of a list, giving weights in ounces (oz) and pennyweights (dwts)—the weights that jeweller uses when he weighs precious metals and especially gold. There was also an envelope with an address on it but most of the writing was unreadable, for it had been crossed out.

After a while, Thorndyke folded these up carefully and replaced them just as he had found them, inside the hat.

There was a loud knock on the door, and a policeman came in, with the landlady and her little boy following close at his heels.

Byramji told the policeman exactly what he had told us. We explained to the policeman how it happened that we were there. We gave him our names and addresses and left.

"Not many clues, are there ?" I said as we were walking home.

Thorndyke looked thoughtful. "There have been three crimes like this one in the last six months, and they all may be the work of the same criminal, the one the police have named "The Camden Killer." They must already have some clues, and perhaps his finger-prints. That's something I must find out. In any case, the hat we've been looking at will help them a lot."

"How ?" I asked. "It'll tell them the size of the man's head, but will that help ? Millions of men wear a hat that size. How else can the hat help ?"

"Don't forget what we found inside the hat," he said, and then he fell silent. I left him to his thoughts and went home, for I had work to do.

As soon as I was free, I went to see Thorndyke as I was eager to know what he had discovered. He was a quick worker and, in a case of murder, allowed himself no rest until the murderer had been caught. When I entered his study room, which was also his laboratory, he was busy at his microscope and there was a glass test-tube filled with a dirty-looking liquid close at hand, on his bench. On his table there was a great pile of books and I noticed that they were all postoffice directories giving the names and addresses of all kinds of businessmen in all parts of London.

"I see you've been examining the dust you got from the hat," I said. "Have you learnt anything from it ?"

"Not much. Sit down and I'll tell you what I've found out so far. Well, the hairs from inside the hat are light brown. One of them has the characteristic shape of hair growing at the edge of a bald patch. The dust from outside the hat shows traces of lead and ash—bone-ash, probably."

"Lead ? Perhaps the man is a painter."

"He may be. But I don't think so."

At that moment, there was a loud knock on the door. A tall, well-

built fellow with a pleasant face, despite its broken nose, came in and introduced himself as Superintendent Miller of Scotland Yard.

"They've put me in charge of the Byramji case," he said. "For some time I've been after the Camden killer and we believe that he committed the Byramji murder as well. I've come to ask you if you've learnt anything from the hat—Byramji told me that you were investigating it. I've examined it inside and out but it hasn't given me a single clue. If you've found anything, I'd be glad to know."

'You shall know all that I know,' Thorndyke promised him. "But tell me, have you the finger-prints of the Camden killer ?"

"Yes, I managed to get them after his second murder. I happen to have them with me. Here they are," he said, handing over a photograph of the prints. "I'm afraid that they're poor ones," he went on. "They're so rough that the lines can hardly be seen. They may have been made on a rough surface. Some of the skin seems rubbed off, as if the man had been handling rough metals."

Thorndyke looked up from his study of the prints. "Yes," he said, the lines are far from clear, but I think that I can learn something from hem."

"I wonder if you have any ideas about the crime," said Superintendent Miller, hopefully. "I'd like to know what you think."

"I don't know anything definite," Thorndyke told him, "but I was thinking that it would be a good idea to call on the people who live at 51 Clifford's Inn. Someone there may be able to tell us something. If you'd like to come with me...... ."

"Oh, I would. When are you going ?"

"Shall we say tomorrow afternoon at three o'clock ? Will that suit you ?"

"Good. I'll be at your place at three."

After Miller had left, Thorndyke sat down and wrote two letters. As for me, I sat down and thought. "Clifford's Inn ? How on earth has he been able to make "Cliffords Inn" out of the "-n" that was on the envelope inside the hat ? How can

Clifford's Inn be connected with the killer ? I knew the place well. It was not an inn or a hotel as you might imagine, but an old building that had been divided into flats, offices, studios and workrooms of various kinds. How on earth could Clifford's Inn have anything to do with the crime ?

Thorndyke said nothing to me about the letters he was writing and I asked no questions. But I saw from the envelopes that he had written to a Mr. F.R. Crayson, a mining engineer, and to a Mr. Highley, a metallurgist. I was even more puzzled.

"Well," said Thorndyke at last, "we'll take these to the post and on the way back we'll stop and have a look at Clifford's Inn. You'd like that, wouldn't you ?"

"Indeed, I would."

And so, when we had posted the letters, we stopped at No. 51 Clifford's Inn.

"Is this where the killer is living?" I asked my friend.

"I can't say for certain. It's only a guess," Thorndyke said.

At the main entrance there was a notice :

ROOMS AND OFFICES TO LET

Thorndyke made for the list of tenants just inside the entrance, and stood there reading it. On the ground floor there was, so we read, "Burton and Fielding, High-class Photographers", On the first floor, there was the name, "F.R. Carrington" in fresh white paint. "He hasn't been here long," said Thorndyke. "Look how fresh the paint is!" On the second floor, we read, "Burt and Highley, Metallurgists". Here, the paint was old and faded, and two red lines had been drawn through "Burt". "Burt has left I see," said Thorndyke, "and only Highley is left to carry on the business. I wonder if he lives here or just uses the place as a workshop. And I'd like to know who and what that Mr. Carrington is. Ah, well, we'll leave all that till tomorrow."

I awoke the next morning with a feeling of excitement. What was going to happen ? Was Thorndyke going to work yet another wonder, and find the criminal so soon ? I arrived at Thorndyke's flat before he had finished his breakfast.

"You're in a hurry to see the end of it all, aren't you ?" he said. "Well, this is the programme. We shall now pay a call on Mr. Frank Grayson, a mining engineer whom I know very well. He knows that I'm coming and I rather think that he'll have a nice collection of rocks waiting for me."

"Rocks!" I said, amazed. "What on earth are you going to do with rocks ?"

"Patience, my friend, you will soon see."

We went to Grayson's office. He was out but his clerk handed Thorndyke quite a heavy bag. I looked inside it. It held a number of pieces of rock of different colours. One of these had bright yellow spots on it, and I pointed this out to my friend. "That's the one I want," he told me, and he put it in his pocket. He thanked the clerk and we made for the door.

"Mr. Grayson says that you needn't bring the rocks back," the clerk said. "They're all practically worthless."

Those rocks really puzzled me but I didn't ask again what he was going to do with a bag full of worthless rocks. I just wondered.

Punctually at three o'clock we set out for Clifford's Inn—Thorndyke, Superintendent Miller, I and the bag of rocks. We rang the bell and the caretaker, a thin man with a worried look, came to the door.

"Good afternoon," said Thorndyke in a friendly tone, "we've come about a room. I see that you have some to let." He slipped tip (and Thorndyke's tips were always large ones) into the man's hand and the man's face brightened. "I'd be glad of any information you could give me about the rooms," Thorndyke went on.

"Well, sir, there's No. 5 and No. 12. They're both empty at the moment, but they're small and don't get much sun. Now, there's No 51, that would be better for you, sir. It's Mr. Carrington's, but he has had to leave suddenly. I've just had a letter from him saying that he's giving his rooms up." The caretaker felt in his pockets. "I've got the letter somewhere," he said. "Ah, here it is!" He showed us the letter which ran like this :

Baltic Shipping Co. Ltd.,
S.S. Gottenburg.
July 31st.

Dear Sir,

I am giving up my rooms at No. 51 as I have suddenly been called away. I regret that I have been unable to give you proper notice of my leaving, and I enclose a cheque to cover the rent for the whole month. I also enclose the key.

Yours truly,
T.W. Carrington.

"You are lucky to have the chance of his rooms," the caretaker said. "They are very nice ones—sunny and quiet. And your neighbours are quiet people. There's no one downstairs after working hours. Upstairs, there are Burt and Highley but Burt has gone and Highley doesn't seem to have much business now."

"May we take a look at No. 51 ?" asked Thorndyke.

"Certainly, sir. Here's the key."

Thorndyke unlocked the door, and we found ourselves in the sitting room of the flat. It contained the minimum of furniture, a small table and two chairs,

and in the bedroom there was only a bed, without bed-clothes, a chair and a table.

"The bird has flown," I said.

"But he's left his hat behind," said Superintendent Miller, picking up the black, soft hat that lay on the table. "And it's a good one." He looked inside it and cried out, "Why it's the hat!"

That was true. The hat had a white silk lining and the initials "D.B." in gold letters, exactly as Mr. Byramji had said.

"Ha!" cried Miller, "this time he shan't escape me. The "Gottenburg" calls at Newcastle. I'll arrange for the ship to be held there and I'll go

on board myself and arrest him. I must be off. There's no time to lose. Mr. Thorndyke, I'm very much obliged to you for your help."

Superintendent Miller hurried off though we begged him to stop.

"He's in too much of hurry," said Thorndyke. "He should have waited to learn more about this Carrington. I think that Highley on the second floor knows quite a lot about him, and now we'll go to see whether I'm right or not. Oh, by the way, I wrote to him last night, using the name of "William Polton"—so you can call me "William" he said with a laugh. "Your name, if he asks, is "Stevenson, John Stevenson". This Highley is going to examine the rocks I've brought."

"So that was why you wanted those rocks—William," I said.

"Yes, John."

We went upstairs to Highley's place. To my surprise, Thorndyke did not at once knock at the door but stood outside, examining the gas-meter to see how much gas had been used lately. He gave a nod of satisfaction, and then he knocked.

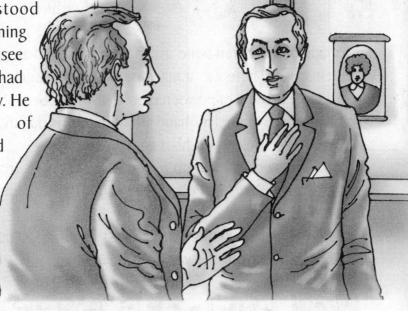

The door was opened by a rather short, stout man in the white coat of a laboratory worker.

"Good afternoon," said Holmes, holding out his hand in a friendly manner. The man shook hands with him, and I noticed that Thorndyke took a good look at the man's hand. "Did you receive my letter ?"

"Yes, I did, but I'm not Highley. Highley happens to be away on holiday and 'I'm doing his work until he comes back in one or two weeks' time. My name is Sherwood. I see that you have brought the rocks that you mentioned in your letter. May I see them ?"

Thorndyke emptied his bag of rocks on to the table. There were quite a number of different pieces and Mr. Sherwood began to examine them through his magnifying glass. While he was doing this, Thorndyke was looking round the room.

His attention was immediately caught and held by the three furnaces there, two small ones and one very large one. Then he looked up at the shelf, which held a row of small white pots—the pots that are made of powdered bone-ash, a material which all metallurgists use in their work. There was a machine for making such pots. There was also a large box full of powdered bone-ash. It looked unusually coarse, and Thorndyke dipped his hand into it to test its quality. Then he slowly wiped his hand clean on his handkerchief.

Mr. Sherwood looked up from his work. "These confirm what you said in your letter, Mr. Polton," he said. "They seem to contain very little gold indeed."

"And what about this one?" asked Thorndyke, taking out of his pocket the rock with the yellow spots.

"Ha!" said Sherwood. "This looks more promising. I should say that there's quite a lot of gold in this."

I was very surprised to hear him—an expert in metals (as

thought) say this because even I, who knew nothing about rocks, knew that it was only a piece of iron pyrites. Any schoolboy could have told him that the spots which shone like gold were, in fact, only a kind of iron. An expert who could not identify iron pyrites! How very strange!

Sherwood took the piece of rock to the window where the light was stronger, and Thorndyke went over to the shelf for a closer look at the pots. He picked one up and, at that moment, Sherwood turned round. When he saw what Thorndyke was holding, he turned deathly pale and shouted :

"Put that down! Do you hear ? Put it down!"

Thorndyke put it down. In fact, he dropped it and it smashed to

pieces on the stone floor. He bent down to pick up a piece that was bigger than the rest. He stood up and held it out for us to see. It was a tooth!

For a moment, no one spoke or moved. Then Sherwood drew a gun from an inside pocket. He was too slow, however. Before he could fire, Thorndyke had thrown a large pot at him. He followed this up with a blow which knocked the man to the ground. I seized his gun while my friend held him down.

"Find a bit of rope," shouted Thorndyke, and I took some rope off a box and tied his feet and knees with it. Now it was impossible for him to run away.

"Tie up his hands, too," said Thorndyke. "I'd like to see what he has in his pockets."

Together we turned the man over. I tied his hands together while Thorndyke searched his pockets.

"Ha!" cried Thorndyke, "this is what we were looking for." He showed me something wrapped in soft white paper, unwrapped the paper, and held out a large and very wonderful ruby.

"Give me the pistol," said Thorndyke. "I'll stay here with him while you go and telephone Scotland Yard. If you can, get Miller before he goes off to Newcastle. Ask him to come here at once. He's a good fellow and we'll let him have the honour of arresting the criminal. He's been after him for months."

It was not long before Miller arrived to arrest the criminal and carry him off to prison.

That evening, Miller was at Thorndyke's flat, waiting eagerly—and so was I—to hear Thorndyke tell the full story of how he had caught the Camden killer.

"The first clue," began Thorndyke, "was the hat with those pieces of paper inside it. There was an envelope with part of an address on it. The address was that of place ending in "-n" London West Central. What West Central places end in "-n" ? It couldn't be "Road" or "Street" or "Square", could it ? It had to be one of the Inns, and it had to be Clifford's Inn because that is the only Inn in West Central.

"Then there was the paper with the weights on it: "3oz 5dwt. Fl—)$\frac{1}{2}$ oz." "Dwt." stands for "penny-weight", and it is a measure of weight used only for jewels and precious metals, especially gold. "Fl—" probably stands for "floor" or "floor sweepings". The dust swept up from the floor of a jeweller's workshop always contains some gold dust. And so it is sent to a metallurgist who separates the gold and sends it back to the jeweller. The first figures– 3oz 5dwt–might show the amount of gold found in the dust from a jeweller's work-bench.

"From this I concluded that a metallurgist was connected with the

crime. And I was sure of this when traces of lead and bone-ash, both of which are used by metallurgists, were found in the dust taken from the outside of the hat."

"Besides this, a metallurgist needs a furnace to melt his metals, and there was a price-list of furnaces inside the hat, you remember."

"All these facts told me where to look and who to look for. I had to find a metallurgist working in Clifford's Inn. The post-office directory found him for me. It showed me that there was only one metallurgist working in Clifford's Inn, and that was Mr. Highley."

"But it was in Carrington's room that we found the hat, the hat the killer took away with him, and not in Highley's," I pointed out.

"Yes," said Thorndyke, "and that brings me to the next chapter in the story. The murderer had been living on the floor below Highley's, under the name of Carrington. That letter of his was a trick. He wrote it to make everyone, the police as well, believe that he had gone off to Sweden on a Swedish ship. And he hadn't. He'd just gone up to the floor above, to Highley's rooms. And that brings us to the question of the hat. The hat was the hat of a metallurgist, no doubt about that. It was

Highley's hat. But where was Highley?"

No one answered. No one could tell him.

"I looked at the gas meter before I knocked at Highley's door," Thorndyke continued, "and that confirmed my fears about poor Highley's end. A lot of gas had been used lately—enough to burn a body in a furnace. That was where Highley finished up. And when I shook hands with the man who came to the door, I saw that he was suffering from a kind of skin disease on his hands—as was the man whose finger-prints you showed me, Miller."

"The Camden killer!" I cried.

"Yes. Sherwood had killed Highley and burned the body in Highley's own furnace. That large furnace of his would burn up everything except the bones and the teeth. The bones were made into bone-ash, that's the powder that metallurgists need in their work. I notice at once that it was unusually coarse. And then there was the tooth."

"When he saw the tooth," I said, "he knew that he was finished."

"Yes," said Thorndyke, "that was the end for the Camden killer."

Since then, every year on August the second, Thorndyke and I have received a box of the finest Indian cigars from Mr. Byramji with his "grateful best wishes".

August the second was the date of the arrest of the man who had murdered his brother and three other men before that—the brutal Camden killer.

THE CASE OF THE STOLEN LETTER

EDGAR ALLAN POE (1809-1849), *American writer and poet, is best known for his short stories, most of which are concerned with horror, violence, murder or the supernatural. His detective stories,* "THE MURDERS IN THE RUE MORGUE" *and* "THE STOLEN LETTER" *(this latter in included in this collection) are among the earliest and best ever written and they have been a model for writers of detective stories ever since.*

5

THE CASE OF THE STOLEN LETTER

EDGAR ALLAN POE

In the autumn of 18—, I was staying in Paris, and enjoying my stay very much. I was near my friend Dupin-Auguste Dupin, the famous French detective. Whenever he had time, we met and he used to discuss some problems of crime with me. This delighted me because I am very interested in crime and criminals. And it made me feel proud to think that the greatest detective in France, and perhaps in Europe, was ready to honour me with his confidence.

One cold, windy evening I was enjoying a quiet smoke with Dupin at his home in a peaceful suburb of Paris. We had been sitting there for about an hour and it was fast growing dark when there was a knock at the door. It was our old friend Monsieur G-, the Head of the Paris police, who had come to visit us. We were glad to see him for we found him interesting though we had little respect for his abilities as a detective. We welcomed him warmly and Dupin crossed the room to light the lamp.

"I hope that I'm not disturbing you," said G- "The fact is that I'd like your advice on a matter

which has been causing us a lot of trouble for quite a while."

Dupin sat down without lighting the lamp.

"Advice? That means we'll have to think. Then I won't light the lamp. I can always think better in the dark."

Monsieur G- laughed. "Another of your curious ideas, Dupin," he said. G- had the habit of calling everything that he could not understand "curious". For him, the world was full of things that were "curious".

"Right you are," agreed Dupin as he handed his visitor a pipe and pushed a comfortable arm-chair towards him.

"What's the matter?" I asked G-. "Not a murder case, I hope?"

"Oh, no, nothing like that," G- said. "It's a simple matter, really. And I'm sure that we can deal with it ourselves. I just thought that you would like to know the details because they are so curious."

"Simple and curious," Dupin said.

"Yes. Well, that is, not quite. As a matter of fact, we are all very puzzled because the case is so simple, and yet it's baffling us."

"Perhaps it's the very simplicity of it that is causing you such difficulty," said Dupin.

G- burst out laughing. He took the words as a joke. "Oh, you do ay the funniest things, Dupin," he said.

"Perhaps you're looking for a mystery where there isn't one," said

Dupin.

"Oh, that's nonsense," G- said.

"Well, what is the matter ?" I asked.

"I will tell you," G- said, puffing at his pipe and settling himself comfortably in his chair. "I will tell you in a few simple words. But I have to tell you, first of all, that the matter has to be kept a strict secret. No one must know of it. I should lose my job if they thought I had told anyone."

"All right," I said. "Go on."

"Or keep it a strict secret, as you prefer," said Dupin.

"Well," began G-, "It's like this. A most highly-placed personage has been to see me personally and has told me that a letter of the highest importance has been stolen from the royal rooms. The person who took it is known. There is no doubt about that because he was seen taking it. It is also known that he still has the letter in his possession."

"How is that known ?" asked Dupin.

"If the thief ever parted with the letter, there would be most unfortunate consequences—that is, if he used it as he is planning to. As yet, those consequences have not shown themselves."

"Give us some more facts," I said.

"The letter gives the possessor great power over a royal personage," G- went on.

"I wish that you would speak more plainly," said Dupin. "Say what you mean in the simplest words you can. I can't follow when you talk in such a mysterious way."

G-, who was enjoying his mystery, went on in the same style, "If a third person, who shall be nameless, got hold of that letter, it would mean the downfall and dishonour of the person to whom the letter was written."

"But who would dare... ." I began.

"The thief," said G-, "is the Minister D-, and there is nothing that he dares not do. He is as cunning as he is daring. This is what he did: The royal personage, to whom the letter was written, was reading it in her sitting room. While she was reading it, the other personage, the one who shall also be nameless, came in unexpectedly. The lady had no time to hide the letter. She just put it down on the table in front of her—fortunately with the envelop on top of it so that only the address could be seen and nothing that was written in the letter. She was most upset and the Minister D-, who entered at that moment, did not fail to notice her confusion. Nor did he fail to guess the cause of it when he saw the letter in front of her. He guessed her secret at once and his look told the lady that he knew all."

"D- stayed there for some time, discussing public affairs with that nameless royal personage. In the course of the discussion, he took a letter out of his pocket and read it out because it concerned the matter under discussion—something about the lighting-up of the streets in Paris. He did not put the letter back into his pocket but left it lying on the table close beside the other one. For another quarter of an hour he stayed on, discussing other matters, and then he stood up to leave. He took the lady's letter from the table, as if by mistake, and left his own there. The lady saw this of course but she did not dare to say anything in front of that third person who was there at her side."

"Then D- has the letter, and the lady knows that he has it," I said. "He has her completely in his power."

"Yes, and he has been using his power over her to further his political ends. The lady knows that she must get that letter back by hook or by crook. She cannot try to get it back openly and so she came to me for help."

"Because you are the cleverest man in the Paris police force," said

Dupin.

"That is what she thinks I am," G- said with satisfaction.

"D- will hold on to the letter, for certain," I said thoughtfully. "While he has it, she is in his power. If he hands over the letter to that other nameless personage, he loses his power over the lady. Then we must suppose that he still has the letter."

"Exactly," said G-. "I feel certain that he has it and so I've made a thorough search of his house. It was not easy because I had to do it in secret. If D- had found out, it would have been the end of me."

"But your men are experts in searching a house in secret," I said. "They ought to be. They've done it often enough," I said."

"Yes, they helped a lot, and so did the curious habits of D-. Night after night he didn't come home at all and so we were free to get on with our search. I have keys, as you know, which can open any door in Paris. Almost every night for three months, my men and I were in his house, looking for that letter. I had to find it. Had I not given my word of honour that I should? And besides, the reward which is offered is immense. I did not stop the search until I was sure that I had examined every possible hiding place in the house."

"Perhaps," I said, "the letter is not in the house, after all."

"I think it is," said Dupin, "because D- may have to hand it over at a moment's notice."

"D- may be carrying it about on himself," I said. "Have you thought of that ?"

"Of course, and my men, disguised as hooligans, have attacked him twice in the streets at night. They've searched him all over but they haven't found it."

"You needn't have done that," protested Dupin. "D- would expect something like that to happen and he'd be ready for it. He isn't quite a fool."

"Not quite a fool," said G- "but he's a poet, and

hat's practically the same as a fool".

"A poet," repeated Dupin thoughtfully. "That's a point to remember."

"Tell us about your search," I said.

"Oh, we were very thorough," he began.

Dupin nodded. "I have no doubt about that," he said.

"We searched each room in turn," went on G–. "Working at night, we gave ten nights, the nights when D- wasn't there, to each one. First, we examined the furniture. We opened evey cupboard and every drawer, looking for some secret section, but my men are too well-trained to miss anything like that. Next we examined the chairs, and the cushions of course. The latter we tested with those fine, long needles that I've shown you, Dupin. We took the tops off the tables........"

"Why on earth did you do that ?" Dupin interrupted him sharply.

"To see if there was anything hidden in the legs. People often hide things there, as they do in the tops and bottoms of bed-posts."

"But surely, you didn't take all the furniture to pieces ?" asked Dupin. "The letter could have been folded up small and pushed into any small hole, in the back of a chair, for example."

"We examined every part of every piece of furniture with a powerful magnifying-glass. If there had been any piece of paper, we should have found it, no matter how small it had been folded. The smallest grain of sawdust would have been as clear as an apple."

"What about the curtains, the bed-clothes, the carpets, the rugs ?" I asked.

"We went over those with the magnifying-glass. And then, when we had finished examining the furnishings, went over the house itself—every square inch of every floor and wall, inside and outside."

"You went to a lot of trouble," I said.

"Yes, I did. But the reward that is offered is very large indeed."

"Did you go over the garden?"

"There isn't one, but there's a yard with stone paving. We went over every inch of this, giving special attention to the earth between the paving-stones. It hadn't been disturbed in any way."

"What about D-'s papers and his books. He has quite a large library, I suppose," I said.

"We went through his papers, every one of them. We opened every book and, what is more, turned over every page. We measured the thickness of the book-covers and studied them through the magnifying glass."

"What about the floors under the carpets ?"

"Oh, we went over them thoroughly."

"And the paper on the walls ?"

"Oh, yes."

"Then," I said, "you are wrong in thinking that the letter is in D-'s house. It can't be."

"I just don't know," said G-. "I don't feel certain. What would you advise me to do, Dupin ?"

"Search the house again."

"Oh, surely, that isn't necessary. We've been over every inch."

"That's my advice," said Dupin. "Take it or leave it." He paused a moment and then asked, "Would you tell me what the letter looks like?"

"Ah, yes," said G-, taking a small note-book out of his pocket.

He opened it and read us a full description of the letter. We listened carefully but said nothing. G- sat with us for a while longer, hoping, I am sure, that we should have something to suggest, but we remained silent. He went away, looking very disappointed.

About a month later, G- called to see Dupin again. It was evening and we were sitting in the dark and smoking our pipes peacefully, just as we had been doing on that evening when G- had called to tell us about the stolen letter.

Dupin offered his visitor a pipe and a comfortable chair, and G- settled himself comfortably. He began to talk about the weather, the theatre and such things, but he was clearly waiting for a chance to speak about what chiefly interested him and what was, in fact, the purpose of his visit.

I gave him his chance.

"Well, G-," I said, "what about the stolen letter? Have you found it yet?"

"I'm afraid not. I searched the house again, as you advised me to, but I found nothing. It was just a waste of time—as I knew it would be."

"What reward is being offered, did you say" ? asked Dupin.

"Oh, a very large one ... a very generous reward..... very ..... I'm not allowed to say how much. But I'll tell you this much: I myself am ready to write out a cheque for fifty thousand francs and give  it to anyone who can bring me that letter. The matter is becoming more and more urgent every day, and the reward has recently been doubled. But if it were trebled, I could do no more than I have done."

"You really will give fifty thousand francs to any one who can give

you the letter ?" asked Dupin.

"Gladly."

"Then kindly write out a cheque for me, for that amount. When you have signed it, I will give you the letter."

I was amazed, and so was G-. He was so amazed that his mouth fell open and his eyes were like saucers. He pulled out his cheque book,

seized a pen and wrote out a cheque for fifty thousand francs. He hesitated then, but only for a moment, and added his signature in great haste. He handed the cheque across the table to Dupin, who examined it very carefully before putting it away in his pocket. Dupin walked over to his desk, unlocked a drawer, took out a letter and handed it to G-. G- snatched it from him, opened it with a shaking hand, and read it through. Then he rushed like a madman out of the room and out of the house, without saying a single word to Dupin and me.

After he had gone, we had to laugh. He had run like a rabbit! When we were serious again, Dupin began to explain to me how he had found the letter. I was all ears.

"The Paris police," said Dupin, "and our friend G- is a good example, are clever in ordinary, everyday cases. They are patient, careful and determined, and in consequence, they are often successful—in ordinary cases. But, and this is important, they have no imagination. You've seen that in G-. He's hardworking, persistent fellow but he has no understanding of people or things that are out of the ordinary. The police here do not try to put themselves in the place of the criminal or to think as he would think. And also, they underestimate his cunning. And so, when G- is looking for something that is hidden, he thinks only of the places where he himself would have hidden it. He did not think that D- had a mind that would work differently from his."

"Now, look at D-. He is a poet, something of a scientist and a bold politician. It follows that he is imaginative, clever and daring, above all, daring. Besides, he is a man of the world and a gentleman of the Court, and as such, he knows how the police work. He would expect hem to search his house and was prepared for it. I am sure that he stayed out night after night to give the police the chance to search the place, so that, in the end, they would give up, convinced that the etter was not in his house. He knew that they would take his furniture to pieces and search every inch of his house for a hiding-place. Knowing this, he would decide to hide he letter in a place that was not hidden out that everyone could easily see. You emember how G- aughed when I said hat perhaps it was

he simplicity of the problem that was puzzling him...... ."

"Oh, yes. He thought that you were joking."

"I was perfectly serious. Some things are too plain for us to see. Perhaps you know of that game that children play. It is played with a map, and one of the players asks the others to find a certain word— he name of a town, a river or a lake, something like that—that is shown on the map. Most children, choose a name that is written in very small etters, for they think that such a word is hard to find. But a good player chooses a word that stretched in large letters right across the map— a word that is, in fact, so plain that it escapes notice."

"True," I said. "That's how it is."

"It is the same with shop-signs in the street," Dupin continued. "We stop and try to read every letter of the small ones, but hardly look at he big ones. Our friend G- never thought that the letter would be right under his nose. He never thought that D- would hide the letter in the

best way, that is, by not hiding it at all.

"I know full well the character of D-, and this led me to expect that he would act as he did. Well, to see whether I was right or wrong, I paid him a visit the other day. D- and I have known each other for years. We've never been friends as I have never trusted the man and indeed, some years ago, he acted very badly towards me—but that's another story. We've always been most polite to each other, and that morning, when I went to see him, he greeted me in a friendly manner. I had put on dark glasses and, at the very beginning of our talk, did not fail to speak of the weakness of my eyes. But, all the same, while we were talking, I was taking good notice of everything around me. The writing-table that stood between myself and the minister had a lot of letters and papers on it, several books and a violin. I noted every item very carefully but there was nothing that made me suspicious. "

"I kept on talking but my eyes went wandering round the room till they fell on something that interested me very much indeed. This was an ordinary, cheap letter-holder, made of wire, hanging by a dirty blue string from a brass hook, just above the fire-place. In the holder there were five or six visiting-cards and a letter. The letter was in a dirty envelope that was torn some way down the middle—as if someone had decided to tear it up as worthless, and then had changed his mind. Instead of throwing it away, he had pushed it carelessly into the top of the holder as something hardly worth keeping. The envelope had the coat of arms of the D-family on it, and it was addressed to D- in a woman's handwriting."

"When I saw this, I knew that I was right. The envelope— there for all to see— held the letter that I had come for. The envelope had been changed and arranged to deceive the police. It did not deceive me. Indeed, its dirty and torn condition and the careless way in which it lay in the holder were so unlike the usual tidy habits of D- that I immediately suspected a trick. It was just what I had expected from D-'s daring nature. He had hidden the letter where everyone could see it. Well, I stayed talking a little longer and then I left. We parted in a friendly manner, and I, on purpose, left my cigarette-case behind me on his table."

"I went back for my case the next morning."

"I beg your pardon," I said. "I see that I am growing more and more forgetful." This led to some talk on the changes that come with age. I was telling him about my weak eyes and weakening sight, when suddenly we heard a gun-shot. Someone in the street had fired a gun. There was a loud scream and shouts from a crowd of people. D- ran to the window, opened it and looked out to see what was the matter. I stepped quietly to the fire-place, took the letter from the holder and put it in my pocket. In its place I put another letter in an envelope that I had carefully prepared at home so that it looked just the same as D-'s torn and dirty one. Then I ran to join D- at the window.

"An old man had fired an old and very rusty gun in the middle of a crowd of women and children. A policeman had arrived on the scene and he was examining the gun. It seemed that he found it harmless, no more than a child's plaything, for he let the old man go with a warning not to do it again."

"I left D-'s house soon afterwards, parting with him in quite a friendly way. On leaving, I went straight to the place where I had arranged to meet the old man. He was waiting for me and asked me if I was satisfied with his performance. "Excellent" I told him and I paid him what I had promised him, and a little more, because the letter was in my pocket."

Till now I had listened without asking any questions but now I asked Dupin, "What made you put another letter in the holder ?"

"I felt sorry for the lady," he answered. "I felt that it was time for her to have her revenge. For months D- had held her in his power. Now she had him in hers. It may be some time before D- discovers that he has not got the letter and he will be acting towards her as if he had got it. Sooner or later, she will be able to trap him and cause his downfall. Besides this, I felt that it was time for me to have my revenge. As you know, D- acted badly towards me some years ago, and I told him then, in a pleasant manner, of course, that I should not forget. Now, he will see that I have not forgotten."

"How ? Did you leave him a message in your letter ?"

"Oh, yes". I felt that it would be impolite not to give him some explanation. And naturally, he would want to know who had got the better of him. He knows my handwriting well, and so in my letter I just wrote these few simple words :

"A trick so bold,
Requires a bolder one to defeat it."

THE CASE OF THE MISSING PLANS

CONAN DOYLE (1859-1930), *is among the greatest writers of detective stories. He is the inventor of that most famous detective, Sherlock Holmes, and of his faithful friend, Dr. Watson. Holmes is able to solve the deepest mysteries in original and brilliant fashion. This can be seen in the two stories in this collection :*

"THE CASE OF THE REIGATE MURDER" and "THE CASE OF THE MISSING PLANS."

6

THE CASE OF THE MISSING PLANS

CONAN DOYLE

It was the third week in November and, as often happens at that time, a thick, yellow fog had settled down on London. From Monday to Thursday, my friend, the famous detective Sherlock Holmes, and I could scarcely see the houses opposite ours in Baker Street. On the first day of the fog, Sherlock Holmes had found plenty to do, sorting out his papers. On the second and the third, he had given his time to his hobby—the music of the Middle Ages. But on the fourth day, when our windows still showed us nothing beyond that "pea-soup" of a fog, Holmes could bear it no longer. His patience was at an end. When breakfast was over, he began pacing restlessly to and fro in the sitting room, biting his nails and tapping the furniture, inwardly raging against his forced inactivity.

"Anything interesting in the papers, Watson ?" he asked impatiently.

I looked. There was the news of a revolution, of a change of government and of a new war, but these were not the things that Holmes found interesting. What he meant was : Was there any news of an interesting crime ? I had to say that there was not. At this he groaned and said,

"The London criminal is a stupid fellow, Watson. On such

a day as this, a murderer could roam about the city, killing at will, as freely as a tiger in the jungle. No one would see him, except his victim, and he would have no trouble in escaping." He paused and then added, with a twisted smile, "It is lucky that I am a detective and not a criminal."

"It is, indeed," I agreed heartily.

"There are at least fifty criminals who are waiting for an opportunity to murder me. What a chance for them if they met me in this fog!" He yawned. "Heavens, how boring it is!" He yawned again.

At that instant the door-bell rang.

"Ha!" he cried. "Let's hope that here is something interesting."

The maid came in with a telegram. He tore it open, and then, to my astonishment, he burst out laughing. "Well, well! Would you

believe it ?" he said. "My brother Mycroft is coming here."

"Why not ?" I asked. "What's funny in that ?"

"Doesn't he say why he's coming ?" I asked.

Holmes handed me his brother's telegram. It ran :

"Must see you over Cadogan-West. Coming at once. Mycroft."

"Cadogan-West ?" I said. "I've seen that name somewhere recently."

Holmes was still thinking of his brother. "How extraordinary that Mycroft should be coming here! It is as if a planet should leave its orbit." And then he asked me, "I never told you about Mycroft's job, did I ?"

"Once you mentioned that he was in government service."

"Indeed, he is. He is in the Secret Service—not one of their active agents, travelling here and there, but their chief advisor. You see, he had such a marvellous memory for facts that he can immediately supply any information they need. And he is now on his way here. What on earth can it mean ? Who is this Cadogan West, and how is he connected with my brother ?"

I searched among the newspapers that littered the sofa. "Cadogan-West, Cadogan-West..... ah, here he is! He is the young man who was found dead on the Underground on Tuesday morning."

Holmes sat up straight, his pipe half-way to his lips.

"This must be serious, Watson," he said. "A death which has caused my brother to change his habits must have something extraordinary about it. And yet the case seemed an ordinary one—from what I remember of it. The young man fell out of a train and killed himself. He had not been robbed. Nor was murder suspected, if I remember rightly."

"From what yesterday's paper says, it seems that some new facts have come to light," I told him, "It seems a curious case."

"A most extraordinary one, judging from my brother's behaviour." He settled himself comfortably in his arm-chair. "Now, Watson," he said, "let us have the facts."

"The man's name was Arthur Cadogan-West," I began. "He was twenty-seven, unmarried and a junior clerk at the arsenal in Woolwich."

"Ha! In government service, I see. That is how he is connected with my brother."

"West left Woolwich suddenly on Monday night," I went on. "The last person to see him alive was his fiancee, whom he left, without a word of explanation, at seven-thirty that evening. There was no quarrel

between them and they were on their way to the theatre at the time. She can give no reason for his suddenly leaving her. The next thing that was heard of him was that his body had been found on the railway line, not far from Aldgate Station."

"When ?"

"At six o'clock on Tuesday morning. The body lay at a curve in the line, at the spot where the line comes out of the tunnel into the open. The head was badly crushed, probably in consequence of his falling from the train."

"I see," said Holmes. "That's quite clear. The man, dead or alive, fell or was thrown from the train. Where did he get on the train ?"

"That isn't known. No ticket was found on him."

"No ticket ? Dear me, Watson, that's strange. Did someone take his ticket in order to hide which station he came from ? That is possible. Or did he drop it in the carriage ? That also is possible. It is strange. He had not been robbed...... ."

"No, he hadn't been robbed. His purse was in his pocket, with two pounds, five shillings in it. His cheque-book was there, as well—it was through this that the police were able to identify the body. There were also two

tickets for the theatre at Woolwich that evening. And there was a small packet of technical papers."

"Ha! Technical papers," said Holmes. "Now the connection is clear: British Government—the arsenal at Woolwich—technical papers—brother Mycroft."

There was the sound of footsteps on the stairs.

"Here's my brother Mycroft," Sherlock Holmes said. "He can tell us all about it."

A moment later Mycroft Holmes came into the room, a portly figure but one that gave, as Sherlock's did, an impression of immense energy. He was followed by a tall, thin, austere man, an old friend of ours, Lestrade of Scotland Yard. Both men looked exceedingly grave. Mycroft sank into a chair and said :

"This is a bad business, Sherlock, very bad. There's nothing in the world that I dislike so much as having to change my habits, but I have had to. It is a real crisis. I have never seen the Prime Minister so upset. As for the Admiralty—it is buzzing like an overturned bee-hive. Have you read about the case ?"

"Something. What were those technical papers ?" asked Sherlock Holmes.

"Ha! That's just the point," Mycroft Holmes said in a very grave tone. "They were the plans of the Bruce-Partington submarine. You've heard of that, surely ?"

"The name. Nothing more than that," answered his brother.

"My dear fellow, it's the very latest invention and the plans were a top secret, of course. They are kept in the arsenal at Woolwich, in specially-built safe, in an office fitted with burglarproof doors and windows. No one is allowed to take the papers out of the office, and yet, here we find them, in the pocket of a junior clerk in the heart of London! It's awful! If the newspapers hear of it, there'll be a public scandal."

"But if the papers were in his pocket, you've got them back, haven't you ?"

"No, Sherlock, no! That's the awful part of it. We haven't got them back. Ten papers were stolen from Woolwich. Only seven were found in that fellow's pocket. The three most important ones are gone.......stolen.....disappeared! Sherlock, you must give up your little puzzles and help us. This is a problem of the most vital importance for the country, and you must solve it for us. It is your duty, Sherlock. Find an answer to these questions : Why did Cadogan-West take the papers; where are the three missing ones; how did the fellow die; how did his body come to be on the railway line; how can the papers be recovered ? Find this out, and you will do your country a great service.

"Why don't you solve the mystery, yourself, Mycroft ? You have all the facts."

"True, Sherlock, but I work from my arm-chair. I can't run here and there, asking railwaymen questions. Nor can I lie, flat on my face, with a magnifying glass in my hand. That's not for me. You are the one to solve this mystery."

Sherlock Holmes smiled. "Well," he said, "since the case appears to be so interesting. I'll have a try. May I have some more details, please?"

"That most important ones, said Mycroft, "I've written down for you on this piece of paper, and you'll find some useful addresses there, too. The man in charge of the papers is Sir James Walter, the Head of the Submarine Department. He has been in government service for more than thirty years and has proved himself absolutely trustworthy. He is one of the two men who have the keys of the safe where the papers are kept. He is the only man who has the three important keys—the key of the outer door, the key of the safe. When Sir James left for London, at three o'clock on Monday, he took the three keys with him. He was at Admiral Sinclair's place for the whole of that evening."

"Who's the other man with a key to the safe ?"

"The senior clerk, Mr. Sidney Johnson, a man of forty, married, with five children. He's a silent, unsociable man, unpopular in the office, but with an excellent record in public service. He was at home the whole of Monday evening, and his key never left his watch-chain."

"Let's hear something about Cadogan-West."

"He's been working at the arsenal for ten years and has worked well. He's shown himself to be honest and reliable—though a bit hot-headed at times. There's absolutely nothing against him. He was the junior clerk and only he and Johnson were able to get at the plans when they needed to."

"Who locked the plans up that night ?"

"Johnson, the senior clerk."

"Then young West must have taken the plans. After all, they were found on him."

"Perhaps," said Mycroft. "But why did he take them ?"

"To sell them," his brother said. "That's why he went to London— to sell them to a spy."

"But he hadn't got the key of the safe," objected Mycroft.

"He had a false key."

"Three false keys then, for he would need the three to get at the papers."

"All right, three false keys," said Sherlock Holmes. "He went to London to sell the papers to a spy. His plan was to copy the papers and bring back the original ones—which he would put in the safe the next morning, before they were missed. But he never returned from London. He was killed on his way back to Woolwich."

"But he wasn't on his way back to Woolwich, Sherlock. His body was found at Aldgate and the Woolwich train doesn't pass there."

"Ha! That's interesting," admitted his brother.

"Besides," went on Mycroft, "if he had planned to go to London to meet the spy that Monday evening, why did he buy two tickets for the theatre and set out with his fiancee for the theatre ?"

"A trick," said Lestrade, who till now had listened with great interest but had said nothing.

"A strange one then," Mycroft told him. "And, Sherlock, if he was going to bring the papers back, as you say, why did he have only seven in his pocket ? Where were the other three ? Besides, if he had sold the papers, You'd expect him to have a lot of money on him, and he had very little."

"I think I know what happened," said Lestrade. "He took the papers to London to sell. He saw the spy. They quarrelled over the price and West came home without selling the plans. The agent followed him, got on the same train, murdered him and took the three most important papers. He threw the dead body on the railway line. That explains everything I think."

"Why was there no ticket ?" asked Sherlock Holmes.

"The ticket would give the name of the station nearest the spy's house, and that was risky for the spy. He took it out of the dead man's pocket."

"Good, Lestrade, very good," said Holmes. "But if you are right, the case is over. The traitor is dead. The secret plans are for certain out of the country by now. There's nothing left for us to do. You don't need me and Watson."

"We do, Sherlock, we do," cried Mycroft, in alarm, "There's something wrong with Lestrade's explanation. I can feel it. Do something, Sherlock. Go to the scene of the crime. Speak to everyone connected with the crime. You have never had such a chance of serving your country in all your life before."

"Well, I'll do what I can," Sherlock Holmes promised. "Come on, Watson. Lestrade, are you free to come with us ? We'll begin our investigation by a visit to Aldgate Station. Goodbye, Mycroft. I'll send a report to you this evening, whether I discover anything or not.

An hour later, Holmes, Lestrade and I were standing on the Underground railway-line at the spot where it comes out of the tunnel, just before the station. The station master was explaining, "This is where the body lay. It could not have fallen from up above, for there, as you can see, are only blank walls. It could only have come from

a train, the train that passed about midnight on Monday."

"Did any of the carriages show any signs of a struggle ?" asked Holmes.

"No," answered Lestrade, "I searched them, myself." And then he went on to say, "A passenger who passed through Aldgate Station at about eleven forty on Monday night told us that he heard a heavy thud just before the train reached the station. It was a thud such as a body would make, falling from the train on to the line. Of course, there was a thick fog at the time and no one would be able to see anything. I think......" he stopped suddenly to ask in astonishment, "Why, whatever is the matter, Mr. Holmes ?"

Sherlock Holmes was staring at the railway line at the curve just beyond the tunnel. He was staring and muttering : "Points...... points and a curve.....By heavens, it may be so!"

"What's the matter, Mr. Holmes ? Have you found a clue ?"

"An idea..... an idea has just struck me," said Holmes excitedly. And then, as if speaking to himself, he went on quietly, "After all, there was hardly any blood on the line. From such injuries there should have been a lot of blood." In a louder voice he said, "Well, I think we have finished here. Lestrade, so we need not trouble you any further. Watson and I will go to Woolwich to see what we can discover there."

Before we got on the train to Woolwich, Holmes sent a telegram to his brother. It ran like this :

"Have a clue. Please send at once to Baker Street a list of foreign agents in England, with full addresses.
"Sherlock."

"We should be grateful to my brother Mycroft for bringing us such an interesting case," Holmes said to me in the train. "It really is something extraordinary." His face took on that look of eagerness which it always assumed when we were in hot pursuit of a criminal. How different he looked from that Holmes who had been yawning from boredom only a few hours before!

"What is the clue that you mentioned in your telegram ?" I asked.

"Waston," he said in a grave tone, "Cadogan-West did not fall from the train. He was killed somewhere else. The murderer placed his body on the roof of the train."

"On the roof ?"

"Strange but true, Watson. The body was shaken off the roof at the spot where the train jolts over the points at the curve near the tunnel. There was little blood on the line because the bleeding had happened elsewhere. That explains why there was no ticket. Well..... we shall see." He said no more but sank into thought.

At Woolwich we took a cab to the house of Sir James Walter, the Head of the Submarine Department at the arsenal. The house was a fine villa with green lawns stretching down to

Thames. We arrived there just as the fog was lifting, and a thin, watery sunshine was breaking through. We rang the bell and the butler came to the door.

"Sir James, sir ?" He said in a grave tone, "Sir James died this morning."

"Good heavens!" cried Holmes in astonishment. "How did he die?"

"If you will kindly step inside, sir, I'll call Sir James's brother, Colonel Valentine," said the butler.

We waited in the drawing-room until the colonel came in. He was Sir James's younger brother, a tall handsome man, with blonde hair and a blonde beard, aged about fifty. His grief showed itself in his wild eyes, his flushed cheeks and his nervous manner. "My brother," he said, "was very proud of his good name and that of his department. The shock of the theft came as a terrible blow to him. It broke his heart."

"We were hoping that he could throw some light on this affair," said Holmes.

"He was as much in the dark as you or I," Colonel Valentine told us. "He told the police all that he knew. He thought that Cadogan-West was guilty, but how he came to such an end he could not understand at all."

"And you can tell us nothing that might help us ?" asked Holmes.

"Nothing. And now, you must excuse me. You will understand that the whole house is very upset over this ......" He then left us.

"I never expected that," Holmes said to me in the cab on our way back. "I wonder if the poor fellow died a natural death or whether he killed himself. If he killed himself, was he blaming himself for some neglect, I wonder! Well, we'll think of that later on. Now let us see what we can learn at the Cadogan-Wests.'"

The Cadogan-Wests lived in a small but pleasant house in a quiet suburb of the town. The old mother was too ill for us to ask her any questions. The fiancee of the dead man was there and readily told us all she knew.

"I cannot explain it, Mr. Holmes," she said. "I can't sleep for thinking what has happened. My Arthur would never sell secret plans to a spy. Never! He would rather die than betray his trust. A more patriotic man never walked this earth."

"But the facts, Miss Westbury ?"

"Yes, yes, they are all against him, but he is innocent."

In answer to our questions, the young lady told us that Arthur was not in need of money. His needs were simple and his salary more than sufficient. In fact, he was saving money for his marriage which was to have taken place in a month's time. She told us that Arthur had seemed worried over something, something connected with his work. Quite recently he had mentioned some secret papers. They were, he had said, very important

indeed and a spy would pay a lot of money to get hold of them. It would not be hard for a traitor to steal the papers, he had told her.

Holmes listened to all this most attentively. "And now," he said, "tell us about that last evening."

"Well, we were walking to the theatre and suddenly he dashed off and left me standing there in the fog."

"Didn't he say anything ?"

"Nothing at all. I waited for him for a while and then I went home. Next morning, they brought me the news. Oh, Mr. Holmes, save his honour; it meant so much to him!"

"I shall do my best," Holmes promised her, but he did not sound hopeful.

On our way to the office where Cadogan-West had worked, Sherlock Holmes told me that things looked

very black for West. "You see, Watson," he said, "his coming marriage gives him a motive for the crime : he wanted money. And the idea of the crime was in his head, for he had mentioned it to the girl." He shook his head. "It looks bad," he said.

"But, Holmes," I protested, "doesn't his character speak for him ? And why should he leave his fiancee in the street like that ?"

"Yes, why......why ? That is something we have to find out, Waston. Perhaps Mr. Sidney Jones will be able to help us."

The senior clerk received us with great respect. He looked haggard and ill. "It's bad, Mr. Holmes, very bad," he said. "Have you heard of the death of Sir James ?"

"We have just come from his house."

"The office is upside down. The chief is dead. Young West is dead. Our secret papers are stolen. And yet, when I locked the door on

Monday evening, the office was something to be proud of. It's dreadful. And to think that West did it!"

"You think he did it ?"

"What else can I think ? And yet I trusted him as I trust myself. That I did, sir. So did Sir James."

In answer to our questions, he told us that the plans were in the safe when he had locked the safe and the office at five o'clock on Monday evening. The watchman was on old soldier who could be relied on to keep a good watch on the place. The watchman had seen nothing unusual that night—but the fog was thick.

After Holmes had finished his questioning, we went over the office and Holmes examined the place carefully, paying particular attention to the lock on the safe, the locks on the door and the iron shutters over the window. Then we went outside and Holmes examined the bush which grew just outside the window. Several of its branches had been broken recently and, at the side of it, there were marks showing that someone had been standing there. Holmes asked the clerk to close the shutters. We noticed at once that they hardly met in the centre, so that anyone standing outside could look in.

When we left the arsenal, Holmes was both pleased and excited. He said nothing to me but it was clear that he was well on the way to solving the mystery. At the railway station also, he discovered something useful. The clerk in the ticket-office, who knew Cadogan-West, told us that he had sold West a third class ticket to London on Monday evening, and West had left by the eight-fifteen train. At time, the clerk said, West had been so excited and nervous that he had hardly been able to pick up his change.

"After leaving his financee at seven-thirty," said Holmes, thinking aloud, "West was in a hurry to get to London. But why that sudden hurry? Let us suppose that a spy had spoken to West about the plans and West had refused to have anything to do with him. Let us suppose that West saw that spy on his way to the theatre, followed him and watched the man through the office window. He saw the man take the plans and followed him. Why did he follow him instead of seizing him and shouting for help ? Could the thief have been his chief or someone connected with his chief ? Do you know Watson, I have a feeling that

I am on the right track so far........But then, how did West's body, with seven of the papers on it, get on to the roof of that train ? That's what I have to find out. My instinct tells me that now I'd better try to work from the other end—from the list of names and addresses that I asked Mycroft to send to me."

When we got to Baker Street, the list was waiting for us. Holmes seized it, read it through, and then spread a large map of London on his desk. He studied this carefully and when he looked up, there was a smile of satisfaction on his face.

"Watson," he cried, in high spirits, "I believe I know what happened." He slapped me on the back and said joyfully, "I am going out now but I'll be back in an hour or two. I'm only going to look round a little, for, of course, I'd never do anything important without my old friend, would I ?"

I waited impatiently for him to return but it was not until nine o'clock that I got a message from him. It read like this :

"Am dining at Goldini's Restaurant. Please come at once. Bring with you a jemmy, a dark lantern, a chisel and a revolver."

"A nice load for a respectable citizen to carry through foggy streets!" thought I as I pushed the things into my over-coat pockets. I drove to Goldini's and found my friend sitting at a little table by the door. I joined him there, and over coffee and cigars, he told me what he had been doing.

"Watson," he said softly, "I think that I've found the answers. I think I know who put the body on the roof of the train, and where. The map I was looking at showed me that one of the spies, whose addresses

Mycroft had sent me, was living near the railway line, not far from Aldgate Station. He was a certain Oberstein living in Caulfield Gardens. I have had a look round his place. His back windows overlook the railway line, and, what is more, the Underground trains often stop there for some minutes. Just under his window, Watson! Oberstein dropped the body out of his window."

"Splendid, Holmes!" I cried admiringly. "Marvellous!"

"When I'd seen the back of his house," went on Holmes, "I went round to have a look at the front. I found that Oberstein was not there. For certain, he left for the Continent where he'll sell the plans to the country that is willing to pay the highest price. He hasn't run away, for he has no idea that we are after him. He'll be back soon. But his being away gives us a chance to search his house. Who knows what we may find there ?"

"But we can't search it without a warrant," I protested.

"Warrant ? We don't need a warrant. We're dealing with a dangerous spy, Watson, and I feel we have every right to break the law in order to catch him. Come on. His place is only half a mile away and we can walk there. Be careful you don't drop your load. If you were arrested as a suspicious character, that would be most unfortunate!"

Caulfield Gardens was a row of those houses which are called "Victorian". They were built in the middle years of Queen Victoria's reign, massive and solid buildings, with porches and pillars, and a general air of prosperity and respectability. Children's voices and the clatter of a piano reached us from

the house next door, but Oberstein's house was as silent as the grave.
Fortunately, the fog hid us as we made our way to the back of the house.
It did not take Holmes long to break the back door open. We went in
and climbed the stairs in front of us. Holmes's lantern showed us the
way to a low window.

"This must be it," he whispered. He threw it open and we instantly
caught the noise of an approaching train. With a loud roar, it rushed
past the house.

Holmes swept his light along the window sill. It was thickly coated
with soot from passing trains but, in some places, the soot was rubbed
off. "Here's where they rested the body, Watson. Look at those
blood-stains. Blood-stains here on the stairs, as well. Well,
we'll wait here till a train stops," Holmes said.

It was not long before a train came roaring out of
the tunnel, slowed down when it reached the open,
and then, with a grinding of brakes, pulled up just
below us. It was not four feet from the window sill
to the roof of the carriages. Holmes closed the
window.

"Well, Watson," he cried joyfuly, "I had the
right idea, didn't I ?"

"Indeed you did,"
agreed whole
heartedly.

"Ah, but there
are some
difficulties stil
ahead of us
Watson. Let's go
through the
place to see i
we can find
anything to

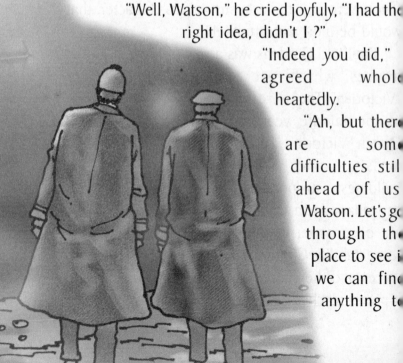

help us."

We searched the kitchen, the drawing-room and the bedroom but found nothing to interest us there. We then went to the study and searched through every drawer and cupboard — in vain.

"The cunning dog has covered his tracks," said Holmes. "He's destroyed, or taken away with him, everything that would show what he has been doing. We'll just see what's inside this, and then we'll go." So saying, Holmes forced open a small tin cash-box that stood on the writing-table. Suddenly he cried, "Eh, what's this ?" He held up some cuttings from the "Daily Telegraph", from that column in the paper where anyone can send a message to anyone else he wishes on payment of a fee. There were no dates on the cuttings but we soon arranged them in order, and this is how they ran :

1. *Hoped to hear sooner. Write to address given on card.— o*

2. *Report unsatisfactory. Must have all details. Money will be paid on delivery of goods.—o.*

3. *Offer will be withdrawn unless contract is completed soon. Make appointment by letter. Will confirm in this column.—o.*

4. *Monday night after nine. Knock twice. Only ourselves present. Payment in cash immediately on delivery of goods.—o*

"Oberstein, signing himself "0", sent these messages to the man who was going to steal the plans and sell them to him, Holmes explained. "Now, Watson, how can we catch the thief ? How ?" He sat for a while, lost in thought, and then he sprang to his feet. "I know, Watson! I know how to catch him. Come on."

We hurried outside.

"Where are we going ?" I asked.

"To the offices of the "Daily Telegraph.""

The next morning, Mycroft Holmes and Lestrade came to Baker Street, and Holmes told them what he had found out. Lestrade shook his head over our crime of the night before, when we had

broken into Obersterin's house and made a search there, without a warrant.

"We police detectives can't break the law as you can, Mr. Holmes," he said. "Your way brings better results but one of these days you'll go too far and find yourself and your friend in trouble."

"We did it for England, home and beauty, didn't we, Watson ? Martyrs, that's what we are!" said Holmes with a hearty laugh. He became serious and, turning to his brother, asked him, "Have you seen O's advertisement today ?"

"What! Another one ?" said Mycroft, somewhat surprised.

"Yes, here it is." And Sherlock Holmes read out :

"Tonight. Same hour. Same place. Knock twice. Most important. Concerns your own safety.—O"

"By George!" cried Lestrade, "if he answers that, we've got him."

"That's what I thought," Sherlock Holmes told him. "Now, if you gentlemen can make it convenient to come with us at about eight o'clock to Caulfield Gardens, we may solve the mystery."

By nine o'clock that night, we were all in Oberstein's study, waiting for our man. We sat there and heard the church clock strike ten o'clock, and then eleven. Our hopes were fast disappearing. Lestrade and Mycroft could hardly sit still, and they were looking twice a minute at their watches. Sherlock Holmes sat with his head bent and his eyes closed. He looked as if he were asleep but, in fact, he was wide-awake. Suddenly, he raised his head.

"He's coming," he whispered.

Soft   footsteps

sounded outside the door. Someone knocked twice. Holmes walked into the dimly-lit hall and opened the door. A dark figure slipped past him. Holmes fastened the door. "This way," said Holmes. A moment later, the man was standing in front of us. When he saw us, the man gave a cry of alarm and turned to run back, but Holmes caught him by the collar and threw him to the floor. The man's hat flew off, and then we could see the man's face. The man was Colonel Valentine Walter!

Holmes gave a whistle of surprise. "Write me down as an ass this time, Watson," he said. "This is not the bird I was expecting."

"Who is he ?" asked Mycroft.

"The younger brother of Sir James Walter, Head of the Submarine

Department," I explained.

Our prisoner sat up and looked wildly around him.

"Who are you ?" he asked. "I came here to see Mr. Oberstein."

"Colonel Walter, everything is known," Holmes said to him, and added, "How an English gentleman could behave in such a way is quite beyond our understanding."

The man groaned and buried his face in his hands.

"We know all," said Sherlock Holmes. "We know that you were short of money; that you had false keys made from your brother's; that you got into touch with Oberstein, who answered your letters through the 'Daily Telegraph". We know that you went to the office on Monday night and that you were seen and followed by Cadogan-West—who had some reason to suspect you. He saw you steal the papers but did not give the alarm because he thought perhaps your brother had sent you for them. Then West, brave fellow and true patriot, followed you in the fog and kept at your heels until you came to Oberstein's house. There, he tried to stop you handing over the plans. And there, Colonel Walter, to the crime of treason, you added the more terrible crime of murder."

"I didn't. I swear that I didn't," the man moaned, overcome with terror and with shame.

"Who did then ?"

"I will tell you all. I did all the rest. I confess, but I didn't murder the fellow, I swear, I didn't."

"Tell us all about it."

"I will. It was like this : When Oberstein opened the door, the young man pushed in and demanded to know what we were doing with those papers. Oberstein picked up the poker and hit him on the head several times. The man died in a few minutes.
There he lay on the floor and

we did not know what to do with his body. Then Oberstein had the idea of putting it on the roof of a train, the next train that stopped outside his back window. But, first of all, he examined the papers I had brought him. He said that three were important and he'd keep them. The others he put in the young man's pocket to make him look guilty of the theft. We waited about half an hour and then a train stopped. We lowered the body on to the roof. In such a thick fog, no one could see us. That's how it was."

"And what about your brother ?" Sherlock Holmes asked the wretched man.

"James said nothing, but I am sure he thought that I had stolen the plans. He's seen me with his keys shortly before. The shame of it was too much for him. He couldn't live with it. He killed himself."

"Where is Oberstein and the three papers ?" asked Mycroft.

"I don't know."

"Didn't he give you his address ?"

"He said that letters sent to the Hotel de Louvre, Paris, would reach him."

"Listen," said Sherlock Holmes, gravely, "if you wish to show that you regret what you have done, you will help us to catch him."

"Oh, I will. I will gladly. Oberstein has ruined me."

"Then sit down and write this letter." Sherlock Holmes then dictated this letter to him :

> *"Dear Sir,*
> *Doubtless you have discovered that an important drawing is missing from the papers in your possession. I am ready to let you have it for the sum of five hundred pounds—to be paid in English notes or in gold. I do not trust the post and therefore beg you to meet me, bringing that sum with you, in the smoking-room of the Charing Cross Hotel, at noon on Saturday."*

Colonel Walter signed the letter and handed it to Sherlock Holmes.

"That will do. I think that will catch him," Holmes said.

It did. Oberstein was arrested in the Charing Cross Hotel and was later sentenced to fifteen years' imprisonment. In his trunk, the police found the Bruce-Partington plans which he was going to sell to the highest bidder.

Colonel Valentine Walter died in prison towards the end of the second year of his sentence.

Sherlock Holmes returned to this hobby— the study of the music of the Middle Ages.

The other week, I learned by chance that Sherlock Holmes had spent a day with royalty at Windsor Castle. He had returned to Baker Street with a fine emerald tie-pin, the gift of our gracious Queen.

QUESTIONS AND LANGUAGE
PRACTICE
THE CASE OF THE SHARP-EYED JEWELLER

QUESTIONS

1. What do you know of William Morris ?
2. What makes an American "the easiest of all to pick out"?
3. Why is Regnier's so well-known ?
4. What was the girl staring at ?
5. Describe the appearance of the man who came into the shop.
6. What did the man want to see ?
7. What did that "most beautiful ring" look like ?
8. When did Morris see that the flower ring had gone ?
9. What was that "dangerous moment" when Morris felt afraid ?
10. What did Morris notice about his second customer ?
11. What had the young woman brought to the shop ?
12. What did she want Regnier's to do for her ?
13. What was the girl's "cunning trick"?
14. Where had the girl put the ring ?
15. What caused the American to rush out of the shop ?
16. Why had Morris felt from the first that the American was a strange customer ?
17. What reasons had Morris for suspecting the girl ?
18. Where had the American put the ring ? How had he fixed it there ?
19. Who had taken the ring from its hidingplace ?
20. How did Mr. Regnier feel about the finding of the ring ? How did Miss Susskind feel?

LANGUAGE PRACTICE

A. Look at these sentences :
     a. It was then that I saw that the ring had disappeared.
        Then I saw that the ring had disappeared.
     b. It was the American who stole the ring.
        The American stole the ring.

Notice how IT WAS gives emphasis to the word that needs it.

Make these sentences more emphatic in the same way. You may have to change the tense of "IT WAS".

1. Then I saw that I had a hole in my stocking.
2. There the accident happened.
3. On April 14th they left for London.
4. William Morris found the ring for Mr. Regnier.
5. Mary had the best marks.

6. Joe likes chocolates.

B.   Study this sentence :

He searched without finding any trace of the ring.

Notice the form of the word after WITHOUT.

Fill in each space with the right form of the word in the brackets :

1.   He went out without......... a word. (say)
2.   They have little hope of......... a prize. (win)
3.   That's not the knife we use for.........bread. (cut)
4.   She screamed on.........the snake. (see)
5.   By.........a taxi, we reached the station in time. (take)
6.   Joe is ill again from .... (over-eat)
7.   The weather prevented us from.........a picnic. (have)
8.   Mary's father is going to give her a watch if she succeeds in.........her exams. (pass)
9.   The postman is late in.........this morning, isn't he ? (come)
10. I am not very good at.........sums. (do)

THE CASE OF THE REIGATE MURDER

QUESTIONS

1.   What was the cause of Sherlock Holmes's breakdown ?
2.   For what reason did Doctor Watson take Holmes to Reigate ?
3.   What was the "excitement" that Colonel Hayter spoke of ?
4.   What was stolen from Mr. Acton's house ?
5.   Who had been murdered at the Cunninghams'?
6.   Why had Inspector Forrest come to Colonel Hayter's ?
7.   What details of the murder were given by Forrest ?
8.   Where did Forrest find the scrap of paper ?
9.   What had caused the death of William Kirwan ?
10. Why is the scrap of paper an important clue ?
11. Who brought the note to William Kirwan ?
12. At what moment did Holmes show signs of a sudden heart attack ?
13. What mistake did Holmes make in the notice offering a reward ?
14. Who corrected the mistake ? How did he correct it ?
15. What happened when Holmes and the others were entering the old gentleman's room?
16. Where was Holmes ?
17. Who shouted for help ?
18. What did Watson, Forrest and Hayter see as they entered young Cunningham's room?
19. "Drop that!" shouted Forrest. What does the word "that" refer to ?
20. "This is what you really need," said Holmes to Forrest. What does the word "This" refer to?
21. Who came with Holmes to Colonel Hayter's house ?
22. What showed that the note was written by two persons ?

23. What led Holmes to suspect that the Cunninghams had written the note ?
24. What proved that William had not been shot in the course of a struggle ?
25. What proved that the Cunninghams had lied in saying that the killer had escaped through the hedge ?
26. Why had the Cunninghams broken into Acton's house ?
27. Why had Sherlock Holmes pretended to have a heart attack ?
28. Why had Holmes made a mistake in the notice offering a reward ?
29. Why had Holmes knocked the table over ?
30. Why did the Cunninghams murder William Kirwan ?

LANGUAGE PRACTICE

A.   Study this sentence:

He would have heard the thief if the thief had been there.

The sentence speaks of something that might have happened in the Past but which actually did not happen.

Make these sentences express past time:

1. He will visit us if he has time.
2. They will tell teacher if they see us.
3. I shall make a cake if you come to tea.
4. We shall go for a walk if the rain stops.
5. You will break your neck if you fall.

B.   Look at this sentence:

I shall be feeling stronger tomorrow.

Notice the Future Continuous Tense.

Change these sentences so that they express future time.

Alter the underline words given below in such a manner so that they also express future time

1. We are sitting in the classroom now.
2. Miss Wong is giving us a lesson now.
3. The boys were playing football yesterday afternoon.
4. I was watching television last night.
5. We were playing a game on the beach at this time last week.

THE CASE OF THE MISSING CLOCK

QUESTIONS

1. Why was Mr. Montague Egg a successful sales man ?
2. What was Mr. Egg's purpose in going to see Mr. Pinchbeck ?
3. Why was there a lot of traffic on the Beachampton road ?
4. What made Mr. Egg think that Mr. Pinchbeck was not a likely customer ?
5. What "horrible sight" did Mr. Egg see on entering the cottage ?
6. What was the time when Mr. Egg made the terrible discovery ?
7. What did Mr. Egg do before driving to the nearest police station ?

8. What did the "Daily News" of June 22nd report about the murder ?
9. What was the police message that was broadcast on June 25th ?
10. Why was Mr. Egg summoned to attend the trial ?
11. Who was the man accused of the murder ? What did he look like ?
12. What evidence did Mr. Egg give ?
13. What was the baker's evidence ?
14. Who was Mrs. Chapman ? What did she tell the court ?
15. Why was the car's number an "unlucky" one ?
16. What happened while young White was cleaning his motor-bicycle ?
17. When had Barton made his statement to the police ?
18. In his statement, what did Barton say about
a. his relations with his uncle ?
b. the time he had left the cottage ?
19. Where had Barton gone after leaving the cottage ?
20. Who had found Barton ?
21. Why had Barton hurried back to England ?
22. What was happening in court at the back of Mr. Egg ?
23. Why was the lady so excited ?
24. Who was Miss Queek ?
25. Where was Miss Queek driving to on the morning of Saturday, June 18th ?
26. Why did she stop at a garage ?
27. What made Miss Queek certain that the man she saw was Barton ?
28. Why did Miss Queek look at the clock at the garage ?
29. What time was it by the garage clock.
30. Why had Miss Queek not gone to the police earlier ?
31. Why was Miss Queek present at Barton's trial ?
32. What was the reason for the postponement of the trial ?
33. For what reasons did Inspector Ramage go in Mr. Egg's car ?
34. In what ways did the two garages look the same ?
35. What was the important difference between the two garages ?
36. What made Inspector Ramage think that Barton was not guilty ?
37. Did Ramage believe that Mr. Egg was guilty ?
38. Why did Mr. Egg give a sudden cry and stop his car ?
39. Where did Mr. Egg drive to ?
40. What did they all immediately notice about the owner of the garage ?
41. At what time had Miss Queek stopped at the garage for petrol ?
42. What was the "clock" that Miss Queek had seen ?
43. Why had the garage owner taken the clock down ?

ANGUAGE PRACTICE

a. There was no one in the house. Nor was there anyone in the garden.
    This means:
b. There was no one in the house and there was not anyone in the garden.

Change these sentences into the (a) form :

1. There was nobody in the fields and there was not anybody in the woods.
2. There was no one in the classrooms and there was not anyone in the playground.
3. There was nothing on the table and there was not anything in the cupboard.
4. The ticket was nowhere in her pocket and it was not anywhere in her handbag.

B. Study this sentence :

The police car was too small to hold all the passengers comfortably.

The meaning is:

The police car was too small to hold all the passengers comfortably.

From each pair of sentences below make one sentence, like the one given you. Omit the word "very":

1. The road was very narrow. I could not take two lines of traffic.
2. The parcel was very big. It would not go into the basket.
3. Mary was very angry. She would not speak to Susan.
4. Joe is very greedy. He will not give us a sweet.
5. The piano is very heavy. It cannot be moved.

THE CASE OF THE CAMDEN KILLER

QUESTIONS

1. Who is Doctor Thorndyke ?
2. What did Byramji's brother die of ?
3. Who was the visitor that Byramji's brother was expecting ?
4. "It's gone!" cried Mr. Byramji. What did he mean ?
5. How did Byramji know that the hat was not his brother's ?
6. Whose hat was it ?
7. What did Thorndyke do with the brush that Byramji brought him ?
8. Why had pieces of paper been put inside the hat ?
9. What was there on the pieces of paper ?
10. Who was the "Camden killer"?
11. What was Thorndyke doing when his friend went to see him ?
12. What were the books that were on the table ?
13. What did the dust from the outside of the hat show ?
14. Who was Superintendent Miller ?
15. What did the finger-prints show ?
16. What was Clifford's Inn ?
17. Who were the two letters addressed to ?
18. What made Thorndyke think
    (a) that Carrington had only just come to Clifford's Inn ?
    (b) that Burt had left Clifford's Inn ?
19. What did Thorndyke get from Grayson's office ?
20. What did Carrington write in his letter ?

21. "The bird had flown." What did the speaker mean by that ?
22. "What did Miller mean when he said, "Why it's the hat!?"
23. Why was Miller in such a hurry to get to Newcastle ?
24. What did Thorndyke do before knocking at Highley's door ?
25. What did the detective do when he shook hands with Sherwood ?
26. What was Thorndyke doing while Sherwood was examining the rocks ?
27. Why was Sherwood's opinion on the rock with yellow spots a strange one ?
28. What happened when Thorndyke dropped the pot ?
29. Why did Sherwood reach for his gun ?
30. "This is what we were looking for," said Thorndyke. What did he mean ?
31. Why did Thorndyke ask his friend to telephone to Scotland Yard ?
32. What was Thorndyke's first clue ?
33. What made Thorndyke think that a metallurgist was connected with the crime ?
34. How was Thorndyke helped by the post-office directories ?
35. In what way was Carrington's letter "a trick"?
36. Where had Carrington gone to ?
37. Where was Highley ?
38. "That was the end for the Camden killer," said Thorndyke. Explain what he meant.
39. How did Mr. Byramji show that he was grateful to Thorndyke ?
40. Why was August 2nd an unforgettable date for Mr. Byramji ?

LANGUAGE PRACTICE

A. Study the form of this question, and its answer :
   You'd like that, wouldn't you ? Yes, I would.
   Make questions of these sentences, following the example.
   Write the answers in their correct form :
   1. You'll come, ...? ....
   2. They've a car,..........................? ....
   3. She's English,...........................? ....
   4. We weren't there,....................? ....
   5. They didn't swim far,................? ....
   6. The boys swam fast,.................? ....
   7. He drives carefully,..................? ....
   8. She doesn't waste time.............? ....
   9. Children loves cakes, ...? ....
   10. She shouldn't lie,....................? ....

B. Look at this sentence :
   We found ourselves in the sitting room.
   Fill in each space with the right word :
   1. They found ......in a large hall.
   2. Mary looked at ....in the mirror.
   3. Tom hurt .... badly when playing football.

4. I kept on telling ....that there was nothing to be afraid of.
5. "You ought to be ashamed of ....," the headmaster said to Tom and John.
6. "Wash.........properly," mother called to Alan through the bathroom door.
7. The cat sat on the mat, licking ....clean.
8. We helped ....to everything on the table.
9. The mice hid .... in their hole under the floor.
10. "Look after......... Tom," his father said as Tom got into the train.

THE CASE OF THE STOLEN LETTER

QUESTIONS

1. Who was Auguste Dupin ?
2. Who was Monsieur G-?
3. "Another of your curious ideas, Dupin," said G-. What did he mean ?
4. Why did G- visit Dupin ?
5. What made G- say, "Oh, that's nonsense!"
6. How did G- know that the thief still had the letter ?
7. Who was the letter written to ?
8. What happened when the lady was reading her letter ?
9. Where did the lady put her letter ?
10. What was the lady's secret that D- was able to guess ?
11. How was he able to guess it ?
12. Why was the lady unable to prevent the Minister from taking her letter ?
13. How could the lady see that D-knew all ?
14. What power did the letter give to D- ?
15. Why must we suppose that D- still has the letter ?
16. Why did G- make a thorough search of the Minister's house ?
17. What made G-'s task easier ?
18. When did G- stop searching the house ?
19. How had G- found out that the Minister was not carrying the letter on himself ?
20. Why did G- expect the Minister to behave foolishly ?
21. Describe how the police searched the Minister's house.
22. What was the advice that Dupin gave to G- ?
23. Why did G- leave Dupin's, looking very disappointed ?
24. When did G- come to see Dupin again ?
25. What was the purpose of his visit ?
26. What did G- hand to Dupin ?
27. What did Dupin hand to G- ?
28. What caused G- to rush madly away ?
29. What reasons did Dupin give for G-'s failure ?
30. Why did Dupin visit the Minister ?
31. Why was Dupin wearing dark glasses ?
32. Where did Dupin see the letter ?

33. What did the letter look like ?
34. Why had Dupin immediately suspected a trick ?
35. Why did Dupin leave his cigarette-case behind him ?
36. What caused the Minister to run to the window ?
37. What did Dupin do while the Minister was looking out of the window ?
38. Why did Dupin pay the old man ?
39. What were the two reasons for Dupin's putting another letter in place of the one he had taken ?
40. What were the "few simple words" of Dupin's message ?

LANGUAGE PRACTICE

Fill in each space with the right word :

1. Are you interested............stamp-collecting ?
2. We had been writing............about 20 minutes when the bell range.
3. This is a matter for the police to deal............
4. He is neither English nor American. As a matter ....fact, he is Irish.
5. Mary will never part............her brooch because her grandmother gave it to her.
6. The two young people met............secret.
7. After a while, he stood up............leave.
8. We have to be ready to start............a moment's notice.
9. He had to take the motor............pieces before he could find.
10. You were right............thinking that they would be late.
11. His hobby is quite out............the ordinary.
12. We went out, prepared............rain.
13. Some sums are too hard............us to do.
14. She acted badly............her friend.
15. Instead............talking, you should be working.
16. The letter was addressed............my father.
17. The policeman let the driver go ....a warning to drive more carefully.
18. Teacher is not satisfied............our work.
19. I feel sorry............Jane who is so ill.
20. It is time............us to go to bed.

THE CASE OF THE MISSING PLANS

Questions

1. Why was Sherlock Holmes so restless and bored ?
2. What did Holmes mean when he asked if there was anything interesting in the papers?
3. Why was Sherlock Holmes so surprised at his brother's coming to see him ?
4. What was Mycroft's job ?
5. Why was Mycroft coming to see his brother ?
6. What did the newspapers say about Cadogan-West ?
7. What was there in the dead man's pockets ?

8. "Now the connection is clear," said Sherlock Holmes. What did he mean ?
9. "This is a problem of the most vital importance for the country," said Mycroft. Explain what he meant.
10. What were the questions to which Sherlock had to find an answer ?
11. Why doesn't Mycroft try to solve the mystery himself ?
12. Who are the two men with a key to the safe ?
13. What was Sherlock Holmes's first explanation of the murder ? Was it a satisfactory one ?
14. What was Lestrade's explanation of the murder ? Was this a satisfactory one ?
15. What did Sherlock Holmes promise his brother ?
16. Where is Holmes going to begin his investigation ?
17. What made Holmes stop what he was saying ?
18. What did Sherlock Holmes write in his telegram to his brother ?
19. What was the clue that Holmes mentioned in the telegram ?
20. What was the surprising news that the butler told Holmes ?
21. Who was Colonel Valentine Walter ?
22. What facts did Miss Westbury give Holmes ?
23. What made Holmes say that things looked black for West ?
24. What did the senior clerk tell Holmes ?
25. What things in the office did Holmes examine with particular care ?
26. What did Holmes notice outside the office ?
27. What did the ticket-office clerk tell Holmes ?
28. What gave Holmes the feeling that he was "on the right track"?
29. What did Holmes do on returning to Baker Street ?
30. "A nice load for a respectable citizen to carry through foggy streets!" What was the load? Who was the respectable citizen ?
31. Why did Holmes think that Oberstein was guilty of the murder ?
32. Why was Watson unwilling to make a search of Oberstein's house ?
33. What proofs of Oberstein's guilt did Holmes find on the window-sill ?
34. What made Holmes say, "I had the right idea, didn't I ?"
35. What did Holmes find in the cash-box ?
36. Where did Holmes and Watson go on leaving Oberstein's house ?
37. What was the message the Holmes had put in the "Daily Telegraph" in Oberstein's name?
38. Who were at Oberstein's house at nine o'clock that night ?
39. Who was the man who came in answer to the message ?
40. "We know all" that Holmes told Colonel Valentine Walter. What did they know
41. What did the Colonel tell them about the murder ?
42. How did the Colonel show that he was sorry for what he had done ?
43. What was in the letter that the Colonel wrote at Holmes's dictation'?
44. Where was Oberstein arrested ?
45. What was Oberstein's punishment ?

46.   What happened to the Colonel ?
47.   What was Holmes's reward ?

LANGUAGE PRACTICE

A.   Look at this sentence :
He had not been robbed.

This means the same as :
No one had robbed him.

Change these sentences to the first form :
1.   No one had seen us.
2.   No one has heard of them.
3.   No one invites you to parties.
4.   No one stopped him on the way.
5.   No one will ask her to dance.

B.   Look at this sentence :
He was saving money for his marriage in a month's time.
The 'S, which is generally used only for person, is used in expressions of time.
Fill in the spaces with the right expressions taken from this list :
a month's journey, a week's holiday, a ten minutes' walk, a night's rest, today's newspaper, fifteen years' imprisonment
1.   You will feel less tired after......
2.   From Hong Kong to London by ship is.........
3.   The spy was sentenced to ....
4.   ....contains nothing but bad news.
5.   From my house to school is no more than...........
6.   The doctor advised him to stop work for a while and take.............in the country.